The WAR that Saved my Life

by *Kimberly Brubaker Bradley*

DIAL BOOKS FOR YOUNG READERS
an imprint of Penguin Group (USA) LLC

DIAL BOOKS FOR YOUNG READERS
Published by the Penguin Group
Penguin Group (USA) LLC
375 Hudson Street
New York, New York 10014

USA/Canada/UK/Ireland/Australia/New Zealand/India/South Africa/China
penguin.com
A Penguin Random House Company

Library of Congress Cataloging-in-Publication Data

Bradley, Kimberly Brubaker.
The war that saved my life / by Kimberly Brubaker Bradley.
pages   cm
Summary: A young disabled girl and her brother are evacuated from London
to the English countryside during World War II, where they find
life to be much sweeter away from their abusive mother.
ISBN 978-0-8037-4081-5 (hardcover)
1. World War, 1939–1945—Evacuation of civilians—Great Britain—Juvenile fiction.
[1. World War, 1939–1945—Evacuation of civilians—Fiction.
2. People with disabilities—Fiction. 3. Brothers and sisters—Fiction.
4. Great Britain—History—George VI, 1936–1952—Fiction.] I. Title.
PZ7.B7247War 2015
[Fic]—dc23
2014002168

Printed in the United States of America

1 3 5 7 9 10 8 6 4 2

Designed by Jasmin Rubero
Text set in Imprint MT Std

*For Kathleen Magliochetti, who first
introduced me to England*

Chapter 1

"Ada! Get back from that window!" Mam's voice, shouting. Mam's arm, grabbing mine, yanking me so I toppled off my chair and fell hard to the floor.

"I was only saying hello to Stephen White." I knew better than to talk back, but sometimes my mouth was faster than my brain. I'd become a fighter, that summer.

Mam smacked me. Hard. My head snapped back against the chair leg and for a moment I saw stars. "Don't you be talkin' to nobody!" Mam said. "I let you look out that window out a' the kindness of my heart, but I'll board it over if you go stickin' your nose out, much less talkin' to anyone!"

"Jamie's out there," I mumbled.

"And why shouldn't he be?" Mam said. "He ain't a cripple. Not like you."

I clamped my lips over what I might have said next, and shook my head to clear it. Then I saw the smear of blood on the floor. Oh, mercy. I hadn't cleaned it all up from this afternoon. If Mam saw it, she'd put two and two together, fast. Then I'd be in the soup for sure. I slid over until my bottom covered the blood-stain, and I curled my bad foot beneath me.

"You'd better be making my tea," Mam said. She sat on the edge of the bed and peeled off her stock-ings, wiggling her two good feet near my face. "I'm off to work in a bit."

"Yes, Mam." I pushed my window chair sideways to hide the blood. I crawled across the floor, keeping my scabbed-over bad foot out of Mam's line of sight. I pulled myself onto our second chair, lit the gas ring, and put the kettle on.

"Cut me some bread and dripping," Mam said. "Get some for your brother too." She laughed. "And, if there's any left, you can throw it out the window. See if Stephen White would like your dinner. How'd you like that?"

I didn't say anything. I cut two thick slices off the bread and shoved the rest behind the sink. Jamie wouldn't come home until after Mam left anyhow, and he'd always share whatever food there was with me.

When the tea was ready Mam came to get her mug. "I see that look in your eyes, my girl," she said.

"Don't start thinking you can cross me. You're lucky I put up with you as it is. You've no idea how much worse things can be."

I had poured myself a mug of tea too. I took a deep swallow, and felt the hot liquid scald a trail clear down to my gut. Mam wasn't kidding. But then, neither was I.

There are all kinds of wars.

This story I'm telling starts out four years ago, at the beginning of the summer of 1939. England stood on the edge of another Great War then, the war we're in the middle of now. Most people were afraid. I was ten years old (though I didn't know my age at the time), and while I'd heard of Hitler—little bits and pieces and swear words that floated from the lane to my third-floor window—I wasn't the least concerned about him or any other war fought between nations. You'd think from what I've already told you that I was at war with my mother, but my first war, the one I waged that June, was between my brother and me.

Jamie had a mop of dirt-brown hair, the eyes of an angel, and the soul of an imp. Mam said he was six years old, and would have to start school in the fall. Unlike me, he had strong legs, and two sound feet on the ends of them. He used them to run away from me.

I dreaded being alone.

Our flat was one room on the third floor above the pub where Mam worked nights. In the mornings Mam slept late, and it was my job to get Jamie something to eat and keep him quiet until she was ready to wake up. Then Mam usually went out, to shop or talk to women in the lane; sometimes she took Jamie with her, but mostly not. In the evenings Mam went to work, and I fed Jamie tea and sang to him and put him to sleep, and I'd been doing all that for as long as I could remember, from the days when Jamie still wore diapers and was too small to use the pot.

We played games and sang songs and watched the world out the window—the iceman and his cart, the rag-and-bone man and his shaggy pony, the men coming home from the docks in the evenings, and the women hanging out wash and talking on the stoops. The children of the lane skipping rope and playing tag.

I could have gotten down the stairs, even then. I could have crawled, or scooted on my bottom. I wasn't helpless. But the one time I did venture outdoors, Mam found out, and beat me until my shoulders bled. "You're nobbut a disgrace!" she screamed. "A monster, with that ugly foot! You think I want the world seeing my shame?" She threatened to board over my

4

window if I went downstairs again. That was always her threat to me.

My right foot was small and twisted, so that the bottom pointed skyward, all the toes in the air, and what should have been the top touched the ground. The ankle didn't work right, of course, and it hurt whenever I put weight on it, so for most of my life I never did. I was good at crawling. I didn't protest staying in one room so long as it held both Jamie and me. But as Jamie grew older he wanted to be with the other children, playing in the street. "Why shouldn't he?" Mam said. "He's normal enough." To Jamie she said, "You're not like Ada. You can go wherever you like."

"He can't," I said. "He has to stay where I can see him."

At first he did, but then he made friends with a gang of boys and went running out of sight all day. He came home with stories about the docks on the River Thames, where big ships unloaded cargo from around the world. He told me about trains, and warehouses bigger than our whole block of flats. He'd seen St. Mary's, the church by whose bells I marked time. As the summer days grew longer he stayed out later and later, until he came home hours after Mam left. He was gone all the time, and Mam didn't care.

My room was a prison. I could hardly bear the heat and the quiet and the emptiness.

I tried everything to make Jamie stay. I barred the door so he couldn't get out, but he was already stronger than me. I begged and pleaded with Mam. I threatened Jamie, and then one hot day I tied his hands and feet while he was sleeping. I would *make* him stay with me.

Jamie woke up. He didn't scream or shout. He thrashed once, and then he lay helpless, looking at me.

Tears slid down his cheeks.

I untied him as quickly as I could. I felt like a monster. He had a red mark on his wrist from where I'd pulled the string too tight.

"I won't do it again," I said. "I promise. I'll never do that again."

Still his tears flowed. I understood. In all my life I'd never hurt Jamie. I'd never hit him, not once.

Now I'd become like Mam.

"I'll stay inside," he whispered.

"No," I said. "No. You don't need to. But have some tea before you leave." I gave him a mug, and a piece of bread and dripping. It was just the two of us that morning, Mam gone I don't know where. I patted Jamie's head, and kissed the top of it, and sang him a song, and did all I could to make him smile. "Pretty soon you'll be going to school anyhow," I said, astonished that I hadn't fully realized this before. "You'll be gone all day then, but I'll be okay. I'm going to fix things so I'll be okay." I coaxed him into going out to play, and I waved to him from the window.

Then I did what I should have done to start with. I taught myself to walk.

If I could walk, maybe Mam wouldn't be so ashamed of me. Maybe we could disguise my crippled foot. Maybe I could leave the room, and stay with Jamie, or at least go to him if he needed me.

That's what happened, though not the way I thought it would. In the end it was the combination of the two, the end of my little war against Jamie, and the start of the big war, Hitler's war, that set me free.

Chapter 2

I began that very day. I pulled myself up to the seat of my chair, and I put both feet onto the floor. My good left foot. My bad right one. I straightened my knees, and, grasping the back of the chair, I stood.

I want you to understand what the problem was. I could stand, of course. I could hop, one-footed, if I wished to. But I was far faster on my hands and knees, and our flat was so small that I didn't bother to stand straight very often. My leg muscles, particularly in my right leg, weren't used to it. My back felt weak. But all that was secondary. If the only thing I'd had to do was stand upright, I would have been fine.

To walk I had to put my bad foot to the ground. I had to put all my weight on it, and pick my other foot off the ground, and not fall down from my lack of balance or from the searing pain.

I stood by the chair that first day, wobbling. I

slowly shifted some of my weight from my left foot to my right. I gasped.

Maybe it wouldn't have been so bad if I'd been walking all along. Maybe the little curled-up bones in my ankle would have been used to it. Maybe the thin skin covering them would have been tougher.

Maybe. But I'd never know, and none of this standing business was getting me any closer to Jamie. I let go of the chair. I swung my bad foot out. I pushed my body forward. Pain stabbed my ankle like a knife. I fell down.

Up. Grab the chair. Steady myself. Step forward. Fall down. Up. Try again. Good foot forward first this time. A quick gasp, a swinging of the bad foot, and then—crash.

The skin on the bottom of my bad foot ripped. Blood smeared across the floor. After a while, I couldn't take it anymore. I dropped to my knees, shaking, and I got a rag and wiped up the mess.

That was the first day. The second day was worse. The second day my good foot and leg hurt too. It was hard to straighten my legs. I had bruises on my knees from falling, and the sores on my bad foot hadn't healed. The second day all I did was stand, holding the chair. I stood while I looked out my window. I practiced moving my weight from one foot to the other. Then I lay down on the bed and sobbed from the hurt and from exhaustion.

I kept it secret, of course. I didn't want Mam to know until I was good at walking, and I didn't trust Jamie not to tell her. I suppose I could have shouted the news down to the street, but what good would that have done? I watched people out my window every day, and sometimes I did speak to them, but while they often waved, and even said, "Hello, Ada!" they almost never really tried to speak to me.

Maybe Mam would smile at me. Maybe she'd say, "Aren't you clever, then?"

In my mind I went further. After a hard day, when I was holding my leg on the bed and shaking from the effort of not crying more, I thought of Mam taking my hand to help me walk down the stairs. I thought of her leading me out on the street, saying to everyone, "This is Ada. This is my daughter. See, she's not so hopeless as we thought."

She was my mother, after all.

I imagined helping with the shopping. I imagined going to school.

"Tell me everything," I said to Jamie, late at night.

I held him on my lap near the open window. "What did you see today? What did you learn?"

"I went into a shop like you asked me," Jamie said. "Fruit shop. Fruit everywhere. Piled up on tables, like."

"What kind of fruit?"

"Oh—apples. And some like apples, but not quite. And round things that were orange and shiny, and some that were green—"

"You've got to learn the names of them," I told him.

"Can't," Jamie said. "When the shop man saw me he chased me out. Said he didn't need dirty beggars stealin' his fruit, and he ran me off with a broom."

"Oh, Jamie. You're not a dirty beggar." We had baths sometimes, when Mam got to disliking the way we smelled. "And you wouldn't steal."

"'Course I would," Jamie said. He put his hand inside his shirt and pulled out one of the not-quite-apples, lumpy and yellow and soft. It was a pear, though we didn't know it then. When we bit into it, juice ran down our chins.

I'd never tasted anything so good.

Jamie swiped a tomato the next day, but the day after that he got caught trying to take a chop from a butcher's shop. The butcher walloped him, right on the street, and then marched him home to Mam and told her off. Mam snatched Jamie by the neck and walloped him herself. "You idiot! Stealin' sweets is one thing! What were you wanting with a chop?"

"Ada's hungry," Jamie sobbed.

I *was* hungry. Walking was so much work, I was always hungry now. But it was the wrong thing to say, and Jamie knew it. I saw his eyes widen, afraid.

"Ada! I should have known!" Mam wheeled toward me. "Teaching your brother to steal for you? Worthless runt!" She backhanded me. I had been sitting on my chair. Without thinking, I jumped up to dodge the blow.

I was caught. I couldn't take a step, not without giving away my secret. But Mam stared at me with a glittering eye. "Getting too big for your britches, ain't you?" she said. "Get down on your knees and get into that cabinet."

"No, Mam," I said, sinking to the floor. "No. Please."

The cabinet was a cubby under the sink. The pipe dripped sometimes, so the cabinet was always damp and smelly. Worse, roaches lived there. I didn't mind roaches out in the open so much. I could smash them with a piece of paper and throw their bodies out the window. In the cabinet, in the dark, I couldn't smash

12

them. They swarmed all over me. Once one crawled into my ear.

"In you go," Mam said, smiling.

"I'll go," Jamie said. "I nicked the chop."

"Ada goes," Mam said. She turned her slow smile toward Jamie. "Ada spends the night in the cabinet, any time I catch you stealin' again."

"Not the whole night," I whispered, but of course it was.

When things got really bad I could go away inside my head. I'd always known how to do it. I could be anywhere, on my chair or in the cabinet, and I wouldn't be able to see anything or hear anything or even feel anything. I would just be gone.

It was a good thing, but it didn't happen fast enough. The first few minutes in the cabinet were the worst. And then, later on, my body started hurting from being so cramped. I was bigger than I used to be.

In the morning, when Mam let me out, I felt dazed and sick. When I straightened, pain shot through me, cramping pains and pins and needles down my legs and arms. I lay on the floor. Mam looked down at me. "Let that be a lesson to you," she said. "Don't be getting above yourself, my girl."

I knew Mam had guessed at least part of my secret. I was getting stronger. She didn't like it. As soon as she went out I got to my feet, and I made myself walk all the way across the room.

It was late August already. I knew it wouldn't be long before Jamie started school. I wasn't as afraid of Jamie leaving as I had been, but I was dreading being alone so much with Mam. But that day Jamie came home early, looking upset. "Billy White says all the kids is leaving," he said.

Billy White was Stephen White's little brother, and Jamie's best friend.

Mam was getting ready for work. She leaned over to tie her shoes, grunting as she sat back up. "So they say."

"What do you mean, leaving?" I asked.

"Leaving London," Mam said, "on account of Hitler, and his bombs." She looked up, at Jamie, not me. "What they say is that the city's going to be bombed, so all the kids ought to be sent to the country, out of harm's way. I hadn't decided whether to send you. Suppose I might. Cheaper, one less mouth to feed."

"What bombs?" I asked. "What country?"

Mam ignored me.

Jamie slid onto a chair and swung his feet against the rungs. He looked very small. "Billy says they're

14

leaving on Friday." That was two days from now. "His mam's buying him all new clothes."

Mam said, "I ain't got money for new clothes."

"What about me?" My voice came out smaller than I liked. "Am I going? What about me?"

Mam still didn't look at me. "'Course not. They're sending kids to live with nice people. Who'd want you? Nobody, that's who. Nice people don't want to look at that foot."

"I could stay with nasty people," I said. "Wouldn't be any different than living here."

I saw the slap coming, but didn't duck fast enough. "None of your sass," she said. Her mouth twisted into the smile that made my insides clench. "You can't leave. You never will. You're stuck here, right here in this room, bombs or no."

Jamie's face went pale. He opened his mouth to say something, but I shook my head at him, hard, and he closed it again. When Mam left he launched himself into my arms. "Don't worry," I said, rocking him. I didn't feel frightened. I felt grateful, that I'd spent my summer the way I had. "You find out where we have to go and what time we have to be there," I said. "We're leaving together, we are."

Chapter 3

In the wee hours of Friday morning, I stole Mam's shoes.

I had to. They were the only shoes in the flat, other than Jamie's canvas shoes, which were too small even for my bad foot. Mam's shoes were too big, but I stuffed the toes with paper. I wrapped a rag around my bad foot. I tied the laces tight. The shoes felt strange, but I thought they would probably stay on.

Jamie looked at me in amazement. "I've got to take them," I whispered. "Otherwise people'll see my foot."

He said, "You're standing. You're *walking*."

My big moment, and now I hardly cared. There was too much ahead of me. "Yes," I said. "I am." I glanced at Mam, who lay on the bed, snoring, her back to us. Proud of me? Not bloody likely.

I slid down the stairs on my bottom. At the end of them Jamie helped me up, and we set out together into the silent early-morning streets. One step, I thought. One step at a time.

It was interesting to be at ground level. The light was tinged pink, and a faint blue haze seemed to rise off the buildings, so that everything seemed prettier than it did later in the day. A cat streaked around a corner, chasing something, probably a rat. Other than the cat, the street was empty.

I held Jamie's hand on my right side, for support. In my left I had a paper bag with food in it, for breakfast. Jamie said we were supposed to be at his school at nine o'clock in the morning, hours ahead, but I'd figured the earlier we got away, the better. I didn't know how long it would take me to get to the school. I didn't want people to stare.

The street was bumpy, which I hadn't realized from my window. Walking was harder than in our flat. The shoe helped, but by the time I'd made it to the end of the lane, my foot hurt so badly I didn't think I could take a single step further. But I did.

"Turn here," Jamie whispered. "It's not far."

Another step, and my bad foot twisted. I fell, gasping. Jamie knelt beside me. "You could crawl," he said. "S'nobody watching."

"How much farther?" I asked him.

"Three blocks," he said. He added, "Blocks is the buildings in between the streets. We've got to cross three more streets."

I measured the distance with my eyes. Three streets. Might as well have been three miles. Three hundred miles. "Suppose I'll crawl a bit," I said.

But crawling on the street was a lot harder than crawling in our flat. My knees were calloused, of course, but the stones hurt, and the trash and mud weren't pleasant either. After a block I took Jamie's hand and hauled myself upright.

"How come you don't walk, when you can?" Jamie asked.

"It's new," I said. "I learned it this summer, while you were out."

He nodded. "I won't tell," he said.

"Doesn't matter," I said. Already the world seemed huge to me. If I looked up at the tops of the buildings I felt dizzy. "We're going to the country. Nobody minds if I walk there." Of course that was a lie. I didn't know anything about where we were going. I didn't really even know what the word *country* meant. But Jamie gripped my hand tighter, and smiled.

The school was a brick building with an empty yard surrounded by a metal fence. We made it inside and I collapsed. We ate bread dipped in sugar. It was good.

"Did you take Mam's sugar?" Jamie asked, wide-eyed.

I nodded. "All of it," I said, and we laughed out loud.

The air was chilly now that we weren't moving, and the ground felt damp. The roar of pain in my ankle subsided into a deep throbbing ache. I looked up at all the unfamiliar buildings, the scrolls and fancy brick-work, the shingles, the window frames, the birds. I didn't notice the woman walking across the yard until Jamie poked me.

She smiled at us. "You're here early," she said.

One of the teachers, I supposed. I nodded and gave her a big smile in return. "Our dad dropped us off, before he had to go to work," I said. "He said you'd take good care of us."

The woman nodded. "And so I will," she said. "Would you like some tea?"

When we got up, of course she noticed my limp. Limp, nothing, I was staggering, lucky to have Jamie to catch me. "You poor thing," she said. "What's wrong?"

"I hurt it," I said. "Just this morning." Which was true enough.

"Will you let me look at it?" she asked.

"Oh, no," I said, forcing myself to keep moving. "It's getting better already."

After that it was easy. It was the most impossible thing I'd ever done, but it was also easy. I held on to Jamie, and I kept moving forward. The yard filled with children and teachers, the teachers organized us into lines. I wouldn't have been able to walk the half mile to the train station—I was mostly done in—but suddenly in front of me was a face I recognized. "That you, Ada?" said Stephen White.

He was the oldest of the White children; there were three girls between Stephen and Billy. The whole bunch of them had pulled up and were staring at me. They'd never seen me other than through my window.

"It's me," I said.

Stephen looked surprised. "I didn't think you'd be coming," he said. "I mean, of course you've got to get out of London, but our mam said they had special places for people like you."

My mam hadn't said anything about special places. I said, "What'dya mean, 'people like me'?"

Stephen looked at the ground. He was taller than me, older, I figured, but not by much. "You know," he said.

I knew. "Cripples," I said.

He looked back at my face, startled. "No," he said. "Simple. Not right in the head. That's what everybody says." He said, "I didn't even know you could talk."

I thought of all the time I spent at my window. I said, "I talk to you all the time."

"I know you wave and jibber-jabber, but"—he looked pretty uncomfortable now—"we can't ever really hear you, down on the street. We can't make out what you're saying. I didn't know you could talk normal. And your mam says as how you've got to be kept locked up, for your own good." For the first time, he looked at my feet. "You're a cripple?"

I nodded.

"How'd you get here?"

"Walked," I said. "I couldn't let Jamie go alone."

"Was it hard?" he asked.

I said, "Yes."

An odd expression passed over his face, one I didn't understand at all. "Everyone feels sorry for your mam," he said.

There was nothing I could say to that.

Stephen said, "She know you're gone?"

I would have lied, but Jamie piped up, "No. She said Ada was going to get bombed."

Stephen nodded. "Don't worry about walking to the station," he said. "I'll give you a ride."

I didn't know what he meant, but one of his little sisters smiled up at me. "He gives me rides," she said.

I smiled back. She reminded me of Jamie. "Okay, then," I said.

So Stephen White piggy-backed me to the station. The teacher that had given me tea thanked him for helping. We marched in a long line, and the teachers made us sing "There'll Always Be an England." Finally we got to the station, which was overflowing with more children than I knew existed in the world.

"Can you get onto the train all right?" Stephen asked, setting me down.

I grabbed Jamie's shoulder. "'Course I can."

Stephen nodded. He started to herd Billy and his sisters into a group, but then he turned back to me. "How come she keeps you locked up, if you're not simple?"

"Because of my foot," I said.

He shook his head. "That's crazy," he said.

"It's because—because of whatever I did, to make my foot like that—"

He shook his head again. "Crazy."

I stared at him. *Crazy?*

The teachers started yelling then, and we all climbed onto the train. Before the noon church bells rang, the train began to move.

We'd escaped. Mam, Hitler's bombs, my one-room prison. Everything. Crazy or not, I was free.

Chapter 4

The train was miserable, of course. Most of the children weren't glad to be leaving like I was. Some cried, and one got sick in the corner of the car. The teacher assigned to our car fluttered around, trying to clean up the mess and stop boys from fighting and explain for the third or tenth or hundredth time that no, there weren't any loos on this car, we would just have to hold it, and no, she didn't know how much longer, no one even knew where the train was going, much less how long it would take.

No loos, nothing to drink, and we'd eaten all our bread. I poured sugar onto Jamie's hand and he licked at it, like a cat. Meanwhile the world moved outside the windows, faster and faster. If I let my eyes unfocus, the scene blurred and ran past me. If I looked hard at one thing it stood still while I moved my head, and it became clear the train was moving, not the world.

The buildings ended and suddenly there was green. Green everywhere. Bright, vibrant, astonishing green, floating into the air toward the blue, blue sky. I stared, mesmerized. "What's that?"

"Grass," Jamie said.

"Grass?" He knew about this green? There wasn't any grass on our lane, nor nothing like it that I'd ever seen. I knew green from clothing or cabbages, not from fields.

Jamie nodded. "It's on the ground. Spikey stuff, but soft, not prickly. There's grass in the churchyard. Round the headstones. And trees, like that over there." He pointed out the window.

Trees were tall and thin, like stalks of celery, only giant-sized. Bursts of green on top. "When were you in a churchyard?" I asked. *What's a churchyard?* I might have asked next. There was no end to the things I didn't know.

Jamie shrugged. "St. Mary's. Playing leapfrog on the tombstones. Rector chased us out."

I watched the green until it started to blur. I'd been up half the night, making sure we didn't oversleep, and now my eyelids began to settle, lower and lower, until Jamie whispered, "Ada. Ada, *look.*"

A girl on a pony was racing the train. She was actually *on top* of the pony, sitting on its back, her legs hanging one off each side. She held bits of string or something in her hands, and the strings were attached to the pony's head. The girl was laughing, her face wide open with joy, and it was clear even to me that she meant to be on the pony. She was directing the pony, telling it what to do. *Riding* the pony. And the pony was running hard.

I knew ponies from the lane but had only seen them pull carts. I hadn't known you could ride them. I hadn't known they could go so fast.

The girl leaned forward against the pony's flying mane. Her lips moved as though she was shouting something. Her legs thumped the pony's sides, and the pony surged forward, faster, brown legs flying, eyes bright. They ran alongside the train as it curved around their field.

I saw a stone wall ahead of them. I gasped. They were going to hit it. They were going to be hurt. Why didn't she stop the pony?

They jumped it. They jumped the stone wall, and kept running, while the train tracks turned away from their field.

Suddenly I could feel it, the running, the jump. The smoothness, the flying—I recognized it with my whole body, as though it was something I'd done a hundred times before. Something I loved to do. I tapped the window. "I'm going to do that," I said.

Jamie laughed.

"Why not?" I said to him.

"You walk pretty good," he said.

I didn't tell him that my foot hurt so bad I wasn't sure I'd ever walk again. "Yes," I said. "I do."

Chapter 5

The day got worse. It was bound to. The train stopped and started and stopped again. Hot sun poured through the windows until the air seemed to curdle. Small children cried. Bigger ones fought.

Finally we stopped at a quay, but a bossy woman standing there wouldn't let us out. She argued with the head teacher, and then with all the other teachers, and then even with the man running the train. The teachers said we had to be let out, for the love of mercy, but the woman, who had a face like iron and a uniform like a soldier's, only with a skirt, thumped her clipboard and refused.

"I'm to expect seventy mothers with infant children," she said. "Not two hundred schoolchildren. It says so, here."

"I don't care in the least what's written on your paper," the head teacher spat back.

The teacher supervising our car shook her head

and opened the door. "Out, all of you," she said to us. "Loos are in the station. We'll find you something to drink and eat. Out you go."

Out we went, in a thundering herd. The other teachers followed, opening the doors to their cars. The iron-faced woman scowled and barked orders everyone ignored.

It was more noise and rush than I'd ever seen. It was better than fireworks.

Jamie helped me off the train. I felt stiff all over, and I had to go something desperate. "Show me how to use the loo," I told him. Sounds funny, but it was my first real loo. At home our flat shared the one down the hall, but I just used a bucket and Mam or Jamie emptied it.

"I think I gotta use the boys' one," Jamie said.

"What do you mean, the boys' one?"

"See?" He pointed at two doors. Sure enough, all the boys were going through one door, the girls through another. Only now lines snaked out the doors.

"Tell me what to do, then."

"You pee in it, and then you flush," he said.

"What's flush? How do I flush?"

"There's a handle, like, and you push it down."

I waited my turn and then I went in and figured it out, even the flushing. There were sinks, and I splashed water onto my hot face. A girl right in front of me—the shabbiest, nastiest-looking girl I'd ever seen—was using a sink in front of my sink, which seemed odd. I frowned at her, and she frowned back.

All of a sudden I realized I was looking in a mirror.

Mam had a mirror. It hung high on the wall and I never bothered with it. I stared into this one, appalled. I'd assumed I looked like all the other girls. But my hair was clumpy, not smooth. My skin was paler than theirs, milky-white, except it also looked rather gray, especially around my neck. The dirty calluses on my knees stood out beneath my faded skirt, which suddenly seemed grubby and too small.

What could I do? I took a deep breath and staggered out. Jamie was waiting. I looked him over with newly critical eyes. He was dirtier than the other boys too. His shirt had faded into an indeterminate color and his fingernails were rimmed in black.

"We should have had baths," I said.

Jamie shrugged. "Doesn't matter."

But it did.

At home, when I looked out my window onto the lane, across the street, three buildings to the left, on the corner, I could see a fishmonger's shop. They got fish delivered every morning, and laid it out for sale on a thick cool piece of stone. In the summer heat, fish could go off fast, so women knew to pick through the selection carefully and chose only the freshest and the best.

That's what we children were: fish on a slab. The teachers herded us down the street into a big building and lined us up against one wall. Men and women from the village filed past, looking to see if we were sweet and pretty and wholesome enough to take home.

That they didn't think many of us were good value was clear from the expressions on their faces and the things they said.

"Good Lord," one woman said, reeling away from sniffing a little girl's hair. "They're filthy!"

"They'll wash," the iron-faced woman said. She directed operations from the center of the room, clipboard still in hand. "We need to be generous. We didn't expect so many. We've got to do our bit."

"My bit don't extend to a pack of dirty street rats," an old man retorted. "This lot looks like they'll murder us in our beds."

"They're *children*," the iron-faced woman replied. "It's not their fault what they look like."

I looked around. The village girls handing round cups of tea were sort of shiny bright, with ribbons in their hair. They looked like they would smell nice.

"Maybe not," another woman said. "But they're not much like our children, are they?"

The iron-faced woman opened her mouth to argue, then shut it without saying a word. Whatever we were, we weren't like their children, that much was clear.

"Ada," Jamie whispered, "nobody wants you and me."

It was true. The crowd was thinning out. Fewer and fewer children remained. The teachers pushed us together and said nice things about us. The iron-faced woman cajoled the remaining villagers.

A blue-haired old woman put her hand on Jamie's arm. "I won't take the girl," she said, "but I suppose I could manage the little boy."

"You don't want him," I said. "He steals. And bites. And without me to manage him he might go back to having fits."

The woman's mouth dropped into a soundless O. She scuttled away, and went off with somebody else's brother.

And then the hall was empty, save the teachers, the iron woman, Jamie, and me. Mam had been right. No one would have us. We were the only ones not chosen.

Chapter 6

"You're not to worry," the iron-faced woman said, which was perhaps the most ridiculous lie I'd ever heard. She thumped her clipboard. "I've got the perfect place for you."

"Are they nice?" Jamie asked.

"It's a single lady," the woman replied. "She's very nice."

Jamie shook his head. "Mam says nice people won't have us."

The corner of the iron-faced woman's mouth twitched. "She isn't *that* nice," she said. "Plus, I'm the billeting officer. It's not for her to decide."

That meant the lady could be forced to take us. Good. I shifted my weight off my bad foot and gasped. I could get used to the pain while I was standing still, but moving made everything so much worse.

"Can you walk?" the iron-faced woman asked. "What did you do to your foot?"

"A brewer's cart ran over it," I said, "but it's fine."

"Why don't you have crutches?" she asked.

Since I didn't know what crutches were, I could only shrug. I started to walk across the room, but to my horror my foot gave way. I fell onto the wooden floor. I bit my lip to keep from screaming.

"Oh, for heaven's sake," the iron-faced woman said. She knelt down. I expected her to yell, or haul me to my feet, but instead—this was even worse than falling in the first place—she put her arms around me and lifted me off the floor. *Carried* me. "Hurry up," she said to Jamie.

Outside, she deposited me into the backseat of an automobile. An actual automobile. Jamie climbed in beside me, wide-eyed. The woman slammed the passenger door, and then she got into the driver's seat and started the engine. "It'll only be a minute," she said, looking back at us. "It really isn't far."

Jamie touched the shiny wood beneath the window beside him. "'S okay," he said, grinning. "Take your time. We don't mind."

The house looked asleep.

It sat at the very end of a quiet dirt lane. Trees grew along both sides of the lane, and their tops met over it so that the lane was shadowed in green. The house sat pushed back from the trees, in a small pool of sunlight, but vines snaked up the red brick chimney and bushes ran rampant around the windows. A small roof sheltered a door painted red, like the chimney, but the house itself was a flat gray, dull behind the bushes. Curtains were drawn over the windows and the door was shut tight.

The iron-faced woman made a clicking sound as though annoyed. She pulled the car to a stop and cut the engine. "Wait here," she commanded. She pounded a fist against the red door. When nothing happened, she barked, "Miss Smith!" and after a few more moments of nothing, she turned the knob and stepped inside.

I nudged Jamie. "Go listen."

He stood by the open door for a few minutes, then came back. "They're fighting," he said. "The lady doesn't want us. She says she didn't know the war was on."

I was not surprised that Miss Smith didn't want us, but I had a hard time believing anyone didn't know about the war. Miss Smith was either lying, or dumb as a brick.

I shrugged. "We can go somewhere else."

The instant I said that, everything changed. To the right side of the sleeping house a bright yellow pony put its head through the bushes and stared at me.

I could see that it was standing behind a low stone wall. It had a white stripe down its nose and dark brown eyes. It pricked its ears forward and made a low whickery sound.

I poked Jamie, and pointed. It was like something I'd imagined come true. I felt again in my gut the feeling I'd had on the train when I'd seen the galloping pony and the girl.

Jamie whispered, "Does he live here?"

I was already climbing out of the car. If the pony didn't live with Miss Smith, it at least lived next door, and wherever it was, I was staying too. I tried to take a step, but my foot wouldn't allow it. I pulled Jamie over. "Help me," I said.

"To the pony?"

"No. To the house." We stumbled up the stone step and through the red door. Inside, the house felt dark and close. The air smelled tingly. The room we entered was full of odd thick furniture, all covered with dark purple cloth. The walls were dark colors, in patterns, and so was the floor. A pale, thin woman wearing a black dress sat on one of the purple chairs, very upright and rigid, and the iron-faced woman, equally rigid, sat across from her. The pale woman— Miss Smith—had bright red spots on her cheeks. Her hair billowed around her thin face like a frizzy yellow cloud. ". . . don't know a thing about them," she was saying.

"Here they are!" the iron-faced woman said. "The girl's hurt her foot. Children, this is Miss Susan Smith. Miss Smith, this is . . ." She paused, and looked down at us, puzzled. The other children on the train had had name tags, but not us. "What're your names?"

I paused. I could have a new name, here. I could call myself Elizabeth, like the princess. Heck, I could call myself Hitler. They'd never know.

"Ada an' Jamie," Jamie said.

"Ada and Jamie what?" the iron woman said. "What's your last name?"

"Hitler," I said.

Jamie shot a look at me and said nothing.

"Don't be impudent," the iron woman scolded.

"Can't," I said. "I don't know what that means."

"It means your name's not Hitler," the woman said. "Tell Miss Smith your last name."

"Smith," I said. "Ada and Jamie Smith."

The iron woman, exasperated, hissed between her teeth. "Oh, really! Well, it doesn't matter." She turned to Miss Smith. "The teachers will have them on their records. I'll inquire. Meanwhile, I've got to go. It's been a very long day." She stood up. I sat down firmly on the chair closest to the door. Jamie darted into another.

"Good-bye," I said to the iron woman.

"I like your automobile," Jamie told her.

"Now, really," Miss Smith said. She got to her feet and followed the iron-faced woman out of the house. They argued for several more minutes, but I already knew who would win. The iron-faced woman wasn't going to let herself be beaten twice in one day.

Sure enough, the automobile roared away. Miss Smith marched back into the room, looking fiercely angry. "I don't know a thing about taking care of children," she said.

I shrugged. I had never needed taking care of, but I decided not to say so.

Chapter 7

Miss Smith saw a louse in my hair that had not been there before the crowded train ride, not that when I got it mattered to her. In a shrill voice she insisted we take baths, immediately, that minute. She said, staring at my foot, "Can you get up the stairs? What happened to you?"

"Got run over by a brewer's cart," I said. Miss Smith flinched. I went up the stairs on my bottom, one at a time. Miss Smith took us into a white room with a big bath, poured hot water straight from a tap, which was fascinating, and gave us our privacy, whatever that meant. There was soap and thick towels. I took a little cloth and rubbed soap into it, and rubbed my face and neck. The cloth came away gray. I rubbed soap into Jamie's hair, and my own, then turned the tap back on to rinse it out. It was wonderful, the bath. Afterward the dirty water ran out a hole in the bottom of the tub instead of having to be scooped out like at home. Jamie, clean, grinned from inside a white towel. I wrapped a towel around myself and let my hair drip onto my shoulders. "Posh, this place," Jamie said.

I nodded. It was a fine place. I didn't care if Miss Smith was awful. We were used to that with Mam.

Miss Smith knocked on the door and asked us where our things were. I didn't know what she meant. We'd finished the food I'd brought, and I'd left the empty paper bag on the train.

"Your other clothes," she said. "You can't possibly put what you were wearing back on."

The other kids on the train had had parcels. Not us. I said, "We're going to have to, that's all we've got."

She opened the door and looked me up and down. I stuck my right foot behind my left, but it was too late. "Brewer's cart nothing," she said crossly, opening the door wider. "You've got a clubfoot. And you're bleeding all over the floor." She swung her hand toward me.

I ducked.

She froze. "I wasn't going to hit you," she said. "I was going to help you."

Sure. Because she was so happy to have me bleeding on her floor.

She knelt and grabbed my bad foot. I tried to pull

it away, but she held tight. "Interesting," she said. "King Richard the Third had a clubfoot. I've never seen one before."

I made myself think of the ponies. The pony beside the house, the pony running next to the train. Me, riding the yellow pony. I went away into my head and gave myself ponies and that way I could bear Miss Smith touching me.

"Right," she said. "We'll go to the doctor tomorrow, find out what we should do for you."

"He won't want her," Jamie said. "Nice people hate that ugly foot."

Miss Smith let out a short, harsh laugh. "You're in luck, then," she said, "because I am not a nice person at all."

She was not a nice person, but she cleaned up the floor. She was not a nice person, but she bandaged my foot in a white piece of cloth, and gave us two of her own clean shirts to wear. They hung past our knees. She combed or cut the tangles out of our hair, which took ages, and then she made a big pan of scrambled eggs. "It's all the food I have," she said. "I haven't been shopping this week. I wasn't expecting you."

All the food she had, she said, except there was butter on the slightly stale bread, and sugar in the tea.

41

The eggs looked slimy, but I was hungry enough to eat anything, and they tasted fine. When I wiped my plate with my bread she gave me another spoonful of eggs. "What am I supposed to do with you?" she asked.

It was such an odd question. "Nothing," I said.

"Ada stays inside," Jamie offered.

"I take care of him," I said. "You won't have to."

Miss Smith frowned. "How old are you?"

This question made me squirm. "Jamie's six," I said. "Mam said. He's got to go to school."

"He's awfully small for six," Miss Smith said.

"Mam said."

"And surely you're older than he is?" she continued. "Don't you go to school?"

Jamie said, "Not with that ugly foot."

Miss Smith snorted. "That foot's a long way from her brain." She tapped her knife against the edge of her plate. "Birthdays. When? Names? Real names, not this Smith nonsense."

"Ada and Jamie," I said. "Smith. That's all I know."

She glared at me. I glared back. After a few moments her gaze softened. "You really don't know?"

I looked at the eggs on my plate. "I asked once," I said. "Mam said it didn't matter."

Miss Smith drew in her breath. "Okay," she said,

"Jamie's six. You're older. Shall we say nine?"

I couldn't tell by her voice how angry she was. I shrugged. Nine was fine. I knew my numbers, eight, nine, ten.

"I'll write your parents," Miss Smith said. "Lady Thorton will get me their address, and I'll write them. They'll tell me." She looked us up and down. "What does your father do?"

"Nothing," I said. "He's dead." Dead for years, either that or gone. I didn't know which. If I squeezed my eyes shut and concentrated, I thought I could remember him, but only as a sort of blurry shadow. A tall man. Quiet, not like Mam.

"Oh," said Miss Smith. "I'll write your mother, then."

Miss Smith was not a nice person, but the bed she put us in was soft and clean, with smooth thin blankets and warm thicker ones. She pulled the curtain across the window to shut out the light. I was so, so tired.

"Miss," I asked, "whose is the pony?" I had to know, before I went to sleep.

Miss Smith paused, her hand on the curtain. She looked out the window. "His name is Butter," she said. "Becky gave him to me."

"Who's Becky?" Jamie asked, but she didn't reply.

43

Chapter 8

In the morning we slept until the sun was halfway up the sky. Miss Smith slept late too. I could hear her snoring in the room across the hall.

I took Jamie downstairs and fed him bread. I crawled again the way I did at home. I meant to keep walking, but crawling was so much easier.

The main room had a back door. Outside was a little space fenced by a stone wall, and then another much bigger space, also fenced. The pony named Butter stood in the bigger space, facing the house, eyes and ears alert.

I smiled. He looked like he was waiting for me.

Jamie said, grabbing my arm, "You're not supposed to go outside."

I shook him off. "That's over," I said. "Here I can go where I like."

He wavered. "How do you know?"

It was my reward, I thought. For being brave. For

walking so long, for walking away. I got to keep walking forever. I hauled myself to my feet. I would *walk* to the pony.

I toddled and stumbled. Everything hurt. The pony watched me. When I reached the stone wall I sat on it and swung my legs over to the other side. The pony stepped toward me, lowered his head, sniffed my hands, and pressed his neck against me. I put my arms around him. I understood how he got his name. He smelled like butter in the hot sun.

I wanted to ride him but wasn't sure how. His back was a long way from the ground. Plus, the girl I'd seen had had straps or something to hold on to. I stood, holding on to the pony's neck, and took a few cautious steps along his side.

The grass in the field prickled my bare foot. The dampness felt cool on it, and seeped through the bandage on my other foot too. The ground was soft; it moved when I stepped on it. Squishy, like new bread. Trees bordered the field, and their tops waved in the sun. Birds twittered. I knew about birds, we had them in the lane, but I'd never heard so many at once.

There were flowers.

Jamie ran around the field, singing to himself, whacking things with a stick he found. Butter lowered his head again, sniffing my hands. Did he think

I'd brought him something? Should I have brought him something? What did ponies like?

The end of his nose felt soft and warm. I traced my hands up his head to his ears, and the clump of long hair between them. I rubbed his neck, and he sighed and leaned into me again. Then he took a step away and went back to eating grass.

I sat down in the field and watched him. He ate as though eating was his job in life, as though he was saying, "I'm not all that hungry, mate, but I've got to keep on with it, see." He flicked his tail back and forth, then took a step, dragging himself to fresher grass.

I sat and watched him, and then I lay down—I was so stiff, and the warm sun felt so nice—and watched him, and then I fell asleep. When I woke, Miss Smith was standing over me.

"You're sunburned," she said. "You've stayed out too long."

I sat up, stretching. Everything ached. The skin on my bare legs had turned pink. It hurt, but I was used to things hurting.

"Aren't you hungry?" she asked. She sounded cross.

I blinked. I was hungry. Crashingly, achingly hungry. I was used to that too. What was I supposed to say? Did Miss Smith want me to be hungry, or not?

"Why didn't you wake me this morning?" she said. I'd never wake her. I wasn't stupid.

"Come." She reached an arm toward me. "It's gone late. I've got to get you to the doctor, and we need to do some shopping."

"I don't need help," I said.

"Don't be ridiculous," she said, and hauled me up.

I tried to shake her off, but my foot ached so terribly that in the end I let her help me back to the house. Jamie was already inside, sitting at the table eating canned beans and toast. I slid into a chair in the kitchen. Miss Smith thumped more beans onto a plate. "Your bandage is filthy already," she said.

I took a deep breath. Before I could speak, Jamie said, "I told her she wasn't 'sposed to go outside."

"Rubbish." Miss Smith's tone was sharp. "Of course she may go outside. We just need a better system. Those shoes you were wearing yesterday—"

"Those were Mam's," I said.

"I could see they weren't yours," Miss Smith said. "Though I don't suppose you can wear a regular shoe." I shrugged. "Well, we'll see what the doctor says. I've hired a taxi to take us there and then we'll come up with something. Don't get used to it. I can't afford cabs very often."

I nodded, because that seemed best.

It turned out that *taxi* and *cab* were both words that meant automobile. Two rides in two days. Astonishing.

I knew what a doctor was, though I'd never seen one before. This one had funny things like panes of round window glass stuck in front of his eyes. He wore a long white coat like the butcher back home. "Hop on up here," he said to us, patting a big wooden table. Jamie hopped, but I couldn't. "Ah," said the doctor, noticing my foot. He lifted me onto the table.

Mam never touched me unless it was to hit me. Jamie hugged me, but of course he never picked me up. People were all the time touching me here. I didn't like it. Not at all.

The doctor poked and measured and inspected Jamie and me. He made us take off our shirts, and he held a cold metal thing to our chests with tubes that ran up to his ears. He ran his hands through our hair and studied the scratchy places on our skin. "Impetigo," he said. This made no sense to me, but Miss Smith pulled a little notebook out of her purse and wrote something down.

"They're pretty severely malnourished," he said. "Looks like rickets starting in the girl. Lots of sunlight for her. Good food. Milk."

"But what do I do with them?" Miss Smith said. "I've never been around children."

"Feed them, bathe them, make sure they get plenty of sleep," the doctor said. "They're no more difficult than puppies, really." He grinned. "Easier than horses."

"The horses belonged to Becky," Miss Smith snapped, "and I never had a dog."

"Who's Becky?" Jamie asked. I shushed him.

"And what about Ada's foot?" Miss Smith said. "What am I supposed to do about that?"

I tucked my foot beneath me. Miss Smith tapped my knee. "Show him," she said.

I didn't want to. I didn't want them touching me more. My foot was out of sight, bandaged, and I was managing to walk some, and I thought that ought to be enough.

Miss Smith yanked my foot out. "Behave," she said.

The doctor unwrapped the bandage. "My, my," he said, cradling my foot in his hand. "An untreated clubfoot. I've never seen one before."

"I thought clubfeet were rather common," said Miss Smith.

"Oh, yes. Certainly. But nearly always successfully resolved in infancy."

Miss Smith sucked in her breath in a way I didn't understand. "But why wouldn't—" She looked at me and made her voice stop.

Successfully resolved, I thought. My foot was not successfully resolved. It sounded like I'd done something wrong. Mam always said my foot was my fault. I'd always wondered whether that was true.

And *clubfoot.* That was my foot. A clubfoot.

The doctor poked at my clubfoot and twisted it and stared until I couldn't bear it anymore. I thought of Butter, how he smelled so warm and good, how his breath felt against my hand. Instead of going to an empty place in my head, now I could go to where Butter was, and that was easy.

"Ada," Miss Smith said loudly, "Ada. Come back. Dr. Graham asked you a question." She was tapping my face. The doctor had wrapped my foot in a fresh bandage. It was over.

"Are you in very much pain?" he repeated.

How much was very much? What did he want me to say? I shrugged.

"Did you understand what he said about seeing a specialist?" Miss Smith said.

I looked at her. She looked back.

"Yes or no?" she said.

I shook my head.

Miss Smith and the doctor exchanged glances. I felt like I'd said the wrong thing.

"Dr. Graham thinks a specialist might be able to operate on your foot."

I didn't know what a specialist was. I didn't know what they meant by the word *operate*. But I knew better than to ask questions. "Okay," I said.

Miss Smith smiled. "It sounds scary, I know, but it would be a wonderful thing. I'll write to your mother right away, to ask her permission. I can't imagine she'll object. Meanwhile Dr. Graham's fetching a pair of crutches for you."

Crutches were long pieces of wood you stuck under your armpits, so you could walk using the crutches and one good foot. Your bad foot, if you had one, didn't have to touch the ground at all.

Crutches didn't hurt.

The doctor said, "See? I knew she could smile," and Miss Smith shook her head and said, "I don't believe it."

The doctor's place was right in town, near the train station. On crutches I didn't need a taxi, so we walked right down the main street. I walked down the street, bad foot and all, and nobody stopped me. We went into the shops and bought meat and veg and groceries. I went into the shops and nobody turned me out. At one point Miss Smith said, "Ada, would you hand me three of those apples?" I'd been careful not to touch anything up until then, but when she asked I figured it must be okay, and I did it and it was. The shopkeeper didn't even look at me.

The shops had so much stuff in them they gave me a jittery feeling. There was too much stuff to see. And I'd never known anyone to buy as much food as Miss Smith did, all at once. She paid for it too, straight up, with cash. Not a thing on tick. I nudged Jamie, and he nodded. Miss Smith was rich.

On the sidewalk, Miss Smith counted her remaining coins and sighed. She led us into a stern-looking brick shop. The inside was just people standing behind counters. You couldn't tell what they were selling at all.

"What's this place?" Jamie asked.

"It's a bank," Miss Smith said. "You've been to banks before."

I didn't know why she'd think so. I'd never even heard of a place called a bank. Miss Smith scribbled on a scrap of paper and gave it to one of the men behind the counter, and he counted out money and *gave it to her.*

"A money store," Jamie whispered, eyes wide.

I nodded. We sure didn't have one of those on our lane.

We were back wearing our clothes from the day before—we couldn't have gone into town wearing only Miss Smith's shirts—but Miss Smith had washed them so we looked and smelled nice. She marched us into a store that sold clothing anyhow, and bought us each a new set of clothes, top and bottom, and something called underwear, which she said we had to wear from now on—three sets of that—and stockings and then shoes for both of us, Jamie and me.

"I got shoes already," Jamie said, eyeing the stout boots Miss Smith chose. "And Ada, she don't need 'em."

Miss Smith ignored him. The shopkeeper, an unpleasant man with hairy eyebrows, said, "These evacuees is nothing but trouble, isn't they, miss? My missus is that fed up already, she's wanting to send them home. Filthy little rats wet the bed."

Miss Smith gave him a look that made him shut his mouth, except he begged her pardon first. And when we walked out the door I had a brown leather shoe on my good left foot.

A real shoe. For me.

Miss Smith had had to buy a whole pair. The man wouldn't sell her just one. She carried the other shoe in a bag. "We'll save it," she said. "Perhaps someday . . ."

I didn't know what she meant, and I didn't ask. I was getting tired, even with the crutches, and I only wanted to think about the walk home. But Jamie danced in front of me, smiling. "If they can fix your foot," he said. "If they can fix it!"

I smiled back at him. Jamie was such a hopeless fool.

Chapter 9

Another thing Miss Smith did was exchange her old radio batteries for charged ones. Some folks in our lane had had radios, so I knew about them, but, as usual, not close up. Miss Smith's sat in the main room on a glossy wood cabinet. As soon as we got home, Saturday night, she put the new batteries in and started it up. Voices came out, talking.

Miss Smith sighed. "I wanted music," she said. She reached up and switched it off. "I suppose we'll have to hear all about the war, eventually." She yawned and sat without moving.

I thought of the food we'd bought. Apples. Meat. I stood up. "Want me to make some tea, miss?" I asked, by way of suggestion. "Cut some bread and dripping?"

She frowned. "Of course not."

I sat back down, disappointed. I was hungry again. But then, we'd already eaten twice that day, if you counted the bread we swiped in the morning.

"It's nearly time for supper," Miss Smith said. She gave me a sort of a smile, although, like Mam's smiles, it didn't make her look happy. "I'll make supper. It's my job to take care of you."

Right.

But then she got up, and she did make supper. A huge supper. Ham. Boiled potatoes. Little round green things called peas, that came out of a can. Tomatoes, like the one Jamie swiped, only cut in thick slices. Bread, with butter. So many different colors and shapes and smells. The peas rolled around my mouth until I bit them and they squished.

Supper was like a miracle, it was, all that food all at once, and yet Jamie, worn out and cross, refused to touch anything except ham. I wanted to smack him. Hot food and meat. Miss Smith might not want us, but she was feeding us fine. Not to mention, I had a shoe. That meant she didn't mind if I went outside.

"Leave him," Miss Smith said tiredly, when I started to tell Jamie off. To Jamie she said, "You can't have second helpings of anything until you've taken one bite of everything on your plate."

There had been pieces of cloth on the table, folded under the forks. Before she started eating Miss Smith had put hers on her lap, so we had too. Now Jamie took his cloth and used it to cover his head. "I want *ham*," he said, through the cloth.

"You may have more ham after you've tried a bite of everything," Miss Smith said. "You're allowed to dislike food, but not before you've tasted it. And get that napkin off your head."

Jamie hurled his plate against the wall. It shattered. Miss Smith screamed.

I tackled Jamie. I grabbed a piece of tomato off the floor and mashed it between his lips. He spat it at me. "Eat it!" I roared. I grabbed peas and shoved those down his gullet. He choked and gagged. Miss Smith yanked me loose.

"Ada!" she said. "Ada, stop it! You'll hurt him!"

Hurt *him*, when it was him disobeying.

"Bedtime, Jamie!" Miss Smith grabbed his flailing arm. "Bath, then bed!" She pulled him off the floor and carried him kicking and screaming up the stairs.

I'll kill him, I thought. I'll murder him for acting this way.

I found my crutches and got to my feet. I picked up the broken pieces of plate, and the food scattered across the floor. I wiped up the water I'd spilled when I knocked over my glass. I could hear Jamie screaming upstairs. Miss Smith was either bathing him or slaughtering him; either was fine by me.

When I finished cleaning the kitchen I climbed the stairs. Dead easy with the crutches. The screaming had stopped. "I put clean water in the bath for you," Miss Smith said. "Did you finish your supper?"

I nodded. I was still hungry, but my stomach was turning circles and I couldn't eat.

There was hot water, soap, a towel. I already felt clean, but the water was soothing. Afterward I put on new clothes called pajamas, that were supposed to be just to sleep in. Tops and bottoms, both blue. The fabric was so soft that for a moment I held it against my face. It was all soft, this place. Soft and good and frightening. At home I knew who I was.

When I went into the bedroom Jamie was curled into a little ball, snoring, and Miss Smith was dozing in the chair beside the bed. She's not a nice person, I reminded myself, and went to sleep.

In the middle of the night I jumped awake, the way I did when Mam brought home guests. I sat up and clutched the blankets to me. My breath came in ragged gasps.

Miss Smith said, "It's all right, Ada. You're all right."

I turned. She was still sitting in the chair beside Jamie. Moonlight came through the window. Miss Smith's face was in shadow.

My heart hammered. My head whirled.

"You're all right," Miss Smith repeated. "Did you have a nightmare?"

Did I? I didn't know. Jamie lay beside me, his mouth slightly open, his breathing soft and regular.

"Were there bombs?" I asked.

She shook her head. "No. I didn't hear anything, but I woke up too." She held her wrist up to a patch of moonlight. "It's gone three o'clock. I didn't mean to fall asleep here. I've slept in this chair most of the night."

Somehow I could hear her smiling. "I haven't slept well for a long time. Since Becky died, I don't sleep well."

I asked, "When did she die?"

Miss Smith cleared her throat. "Three years ago. Three years ago next Tuesday."

She hadn't slept well for three years?

"It's part of why I didn't want to take you," she continued. "It's nothing to do with you. I'm always so much worse in the fall. And then the days get so short and—well, I'm never very good in the winter either. Never was, not even when I was your age. I hate the darkness and the cold."

I nodded. I hated them too. In winter chilblains covered my hands and feet, and they itched and burned like crazy. I asked, "Was Becky your kid?"

"My *kid*?" Miss Smith gave a bark of harsh laughter. "No. She was my friend. My best friend. We were at university together. This was her house, she left it to me."

"And Butter," I said, remembering.

"She gave me Butter long before she died. She wanted me to like horses, the way she did. It didn't take."

"What killed her?" I asked.

"Pneumonia. That's a sickness in the lungs."

I nodded. Talking to Miss Smith had helped my panic subside. I unclenched my hands from the blankets and lay back down. "You could sleep here," I said to Miss Smith. Jamie was in the middle of the bed, so there was room on her side.

She shook her head. "No, I'll—well, maybe. Just this once." She slid in beside Jamie and pulled the blankets over herself. I pulled my end over myself, feeling again the unexpected softness, the warmth.

The next thing I knew the room was full of light, the sound of church bells was coming through the open windows, and Miss Smith was saying, "Oh, Jamie, you wet the bed."

He never did, at home. I remembered the surly salesman who'd complained about his evacuees' bed-wetting, and I gave Jamie such a glare that he burst into tears.

"No matter," Miss Smith said, though she looked annoyed. "It'll all wash. Monday we'll buy a rubber sheet in case it happens again."

She was all the time having to buy stuff. I said, mostly to ease my worry, "Of course, you're rich." Of course she was, with the posh house and all the food, not to mention a bank to hand her money.

"Far from it," she replied. "I've been living off the sale of Becky's hunters." She stood up, stretching. "What's with those blasted bells? Have we slept that long? I suppose I should be taking you to church, that's what a decent guardian would do." She shrugged. "Too late now."

Downstairs she made tea. She told Jamie to put the radio on. A deep, sonorous voice came out of it, very solemn and slow. Something about it made Jamie and me sit to listen. Miss Smith came in from the kitchen and perched on the edge of the chair.

The Voice said, "As the prime minister announced just a short time ago, England and Germany are now at war."

The church bells had gone silent. Jamie said, "Will they bomb us now?" and Miss Smith nodded and said, "Yes."

Chapter 10

Up until then, that morning, I'd forgotten about the bombs. They were supposed to be in London, not here at Miss Smith's house, but even so I'd forgotten them. You wouldn't think you could forget a thing like bombs.

The squelchy feeling swirled in my stomach again. "What do they mean, we are now at war?" I asked. "Weren't we already? We're here."

"The government evacuated cities ahead of time," Miss Smith explained. "They knew the war was coming, just not exactly when."

"If they knew it was coming, they could have stopped it," I said.

Miss Smith shook her head. "You can't stop Hitler without a fight. Don't worry, Ada. You'll be safe, and your mother will be safe, and I'm sure you'll be able to go home soon."

The way she said it, with a fake smile, told me she was lying. I didn't know why she would lie.

"I hope not," I said, before I thought. I bit back my next words, which were, *I'd rather be here.*

Miss Smith looked startled. She seemed about to say something, but, before she could, Jamie began to cry. "I want to go home," he said. "I don't want a war. I don't want bombs. I'm scared. I want to go home."

When I thought of going home, I couldn't breathe. Home was more frightening than bombs. What was Jamie thinking?

Miss Smith sighed. She took her handkerchief and wiped the tears and snot off Jamie's face. "No one's asking us what we want," she said. "Come. Let's have something to eat."

After we ate, Miss Smith sat beside the radio, looking distant and unhappy. "Miss?" I said. "Have they started bombing yet?"

She shook her head. "Not yet. The sirens went off in London, but it was just a drill."

I perched on the edge of the chair beside her. The voice on the radio droned on. "Miss?" I said. "What're hunters?"

She looked up as though half asleep. "What?"

I repeated the question. "You said you were living off the sale of Becky's hunters," I said. I knew about selling things. There was a pawn shop down our lane, and when work at the docks was slow, women took things there.

"Hunters are an expensive type of horse," she said. "Becky had two of them."

"We could eat less," I said. "Jamie and me. We're used to it."

Miss Smith's gaze sharpened. "Of course not," she said. Her voice took on an edge that made me swallow. "You aren't to worry about that. I'll handle it, or Lady Thorton will. You'll be looked after."

"It's just—"

"You're not to worry," she said. "It's a beautiful day. Wouldn't you like to play outside?"

Jamie was already out there. I nodded, took my crutches, and went. Butter grazed far across the field. "Butter!" I called, sliding over the pasture wall. He raised his head, but didn't come to me.

I lay down. The field was fascinating. Grass, dirt, flowers. Little flying bugs. I rolled onto my stomach and stroked the grass, sniffed it, pulled it out of the dirt. Scooted forward to examine a white flower.

Eventually I felt a whoosh of breath against my neck. I rolled over, laughing, expecting Jamie, but it was Butter. He sniffed my head, then stepped aside, grazing. I watched his feet and how he moved them, and how his long yellow tail swished flies away.

The sun was high and then it was lower, and the air grew chilly. "Supper!" Miss Smith shouted from the house. When we came in she gave me an eye and said, "Have you been rolling in mud?"

I didn't know what she meant.

"Never mind," she said. "Don't look so stricken. You'll wash."

Jamie shouted, "Another BATH?"

"Sit and eat," Miss Smith said. "Yes, a bath. You can plan on having a bath every night while you're here."

"Every *night*?" Mud or not, I felt cleaner than I'd ever been.

"I don't mind you getting dirty," Miss Smith said, "but I won't have mud on my sheets."

Jamie and I looked around. There were lots of things whose names we didn't know. And clearly she *did* mind our getting dirty, at least a little. Finally I said, "Miss? What're sheets?"

Sheets were the thin white blankets on the bed. Supper was something called soup, that came in bowls. You were supposed to drink it from spoons, not from the bowls themselves, which seemed like too much work. But I was hungry, and the soup was salty and had bits of meat in it, so I did as I was told.

Jamie refused to eat at all.

"If you want to go to bed hungry, you certainly may," Miss Smith said. "Soup is all I've made and soup is all there is to eat."

This was a lie and we all knew it. Her cupboard held all sorts of food. But Jamie'd gone to bed hungry before. It wouldn't kill him.

At night he cried into his pillow and in the morning he'd wet the bed again. "I want to go home," he said. "I want to see Billy White. I want to be like always. I want to go home."

I didn't. Not ever. I had run away once and I'd run away again.

Chapter 11

The next week three things happened. First, Miss Smith spent most of each day either sleeping or staring dully into space. On Monday she made meals for us but did nothing else. On Tuesday she didn't even get out of bed. I'd watched her cooking on her range enough to understand how it worked, so I fed Jamie and me. Midafternoon I made Miss Smith some tea. Jamie carried it up the stairs for me and we took it into her room.

She lay on her side, awake but staring at nothing. Her eyes were red and swollen. She seemed surprised to see us. "I've abandoned you," she said, without moving. "I told Lady Thorton I'm not fit to care for children. I said so."

I set the tea on the table by her bed. "Here, miss."

She sat up. "You shouldn't have to take care of me," she said. "I'm supposed to be taking care of you." She took a sip, and fresh tears sprang to her eyes. "You've sugared it," she said.

That was how she took it. One sugar, no milk. I'd watched. "Yes, miss," I said, ducking a little in case she tried to smack me. "Not much, though. There's plenty of sugar left. I didn't take any." Though I'd let Jamie have some.

"I'm not going to hit you," she said. "I wish you'd understand that. I'm neglecting you, certainly, but I won't hit you, and I don't care what you eat. It was *thoughtful* of you to sugar my tea. It was thoughtful of you to bring me tea in the first place."

"Yes, miss," I said. Thoughtful: good or bad?

She sighed. "And we haven't heard back from your mother. Your name is Smith, though. Your last name. Until Lady Thorton told me, I was sure you were lying."

"Yes, miss."

"After that business about Hitler."

I turned to go. I'd had an eventful morning, and I was hungry myself, and could do with some tea.

"It's a common enough name, Smith," Miss Smith said. "But still, I thought you were lying."

She stayed in bed even after she finished the tea. I let Jamie rummage through the cupboard and eat anything he liked, and I did too, though I was pretty sure

I'd get in trouble for it later on. I let Jamie skip his bath, but I took an extra-long one, with hot water so deep my legs floated. I pulled the sheets off the bed so it wouldn't matter that Jamie had wet them the night before, and we slept fine.

In the morning Miss Smith got up, her frizzy hair a yellow cloud around her head. "I'll try to do better," she told us. "Yesterday was—about Becky. I'll do better today."

I shrugged. "I can take care of Jamie."

"Probably," Miss Smith said, "but somebody ought to take care of you."

That was the first thing. The second was that the Royal Air Force built an airfield across the road from Butter's pasture. It went up completely in three days, landing strip, huts, everything. Jamie, fascinated, kept sneaking over to watch, until an officer marched him back to Miss Smith with his hand around Jamie's neck. "Keep him home, ma'am," he said. "No civilians on the airfield."

The third thing is that Billy White went back to London.

Jamie'd fussed about missing Billy and his friends, but I didn't know how to find, and I wasn't going to walk the countryside in a blind search. I'd gotten the hang of crutches quick, so walking was easy, but I enjoyed having Jamie to myself. We were spending our days outside. There was a building in the garden called a stable, that Becky's horses used to live in, and sometimes we played there, but mostly we were in Butter's field, which I loved.

On Thursday all three of us walked into town, because we'd finally eaten up most of the food. The first thing we saw was Billy White with his mother and his sisters waiting at the station for the train.

"Billy!" Jamie shouted. He ran up to Billy's family and grinned at them. "Where're you staying? I'm not far, it's just—"

Billy said, "Mum's come to take us. We're going home."

Jamie stared. "But what about Hitler?" he asked. "What about the bombs?"

"Haven't been any bombs so far," Billy's mother said. She had her arm around her youngest girl. When I smiled at the girl, Billy's mother pulled her a little bit away from me, as though my bad foot might be catching. "And I can't stand it, being away from them," she went on. "It feels wrong. I reckon we'll stick the war out together." She gave me a sideways glance. "'S that you, Ada? Your mum said as how you'd gone too, but

I didn't believe it. Only you weren't at your window."
She looked me up and down, particularly down, at
my carefully bandaged foot. Miss Smith washed the
bandages and gave me a clean one every day.

"I'm not simple," I said. "I've got a bad foot, that's
all."

"I dunno," Billy's mother said, still shielding her
daughter. "Your mam—"

"I've written to her," Miss Smith said, coming up
behind us. "But perhaps you could take a message to
her too. The doctor says—"

Billy interrupted. "I hate it here," he said. "The
people that took us, they're mean as a bunch of starved
cats."

"I hate it here too," Jamie said. He turned to Miss
Smith. "Can I go home? Will you take us home?"

Miss Smith shook her head, smiling, as though
Jamie were making a joke. "I've never even been to
London," she said. "I wouldn't know where to go."

"Home," Jamie insisted.

"Where's Stephen?" I asked.

Billy's mom scowled. "He won't come," she said.
"Thinks he's important, he does." She gave me
another odd look. "I'm that surprised to see you out
with ordinary people. I thought they'd put you in an
asylum."

From the tone of her voice it was clear she thought I should be locked away. The disgust in it stunned me. For years I'd waved to Billy's mother out my window, and she always waved back. I'd thought she was a nice person. I'd thought she liked me. Clearly she did not. I didn't know what to say. I didn't even know where to look. Susan's hand touched my shoulder and I turned a little so that I could see the edge of her skirt. I couldn't stand looking at Billy's mother anymore.

The train came up and Billy's mother herded her children toward it. Jamie began to howl. "Take me with you!"

Miss Smith held him back. "Your mother wants you here," she said. "She wants you safe."

"She misses me," Jamie said. "An' Ada'll take care of me. Mam misses us. Right, Ada? Right? She wants us home!"

I swallowed. Maybe. After all, with me gone she didn't have anybody to fix her tea. Maybe she'd be happy to see me, now that I could walk, especially with the crutches. Maybe she'd wonder why she never thought of crutches herself.

Maybe she'd see I wasn't simple.

Or maybe I was. Maybe there was a reason they kept me shut up in one room.

A wave of dizziness swept me. *Think of Butter*, I told myself desperately. *Think of riding Butter.*

Meanwhile Jamie's screams increased. He kicked Miss Smith, hard, and tried to yank himself out of her grasp. "Billy!" he shouted. "Take me with you! I want to go! I WANT TO GO HOME!"

Miss Smith held on to him until the train had gone.

"I hate you!" Jamie sobbed, flailing his arms and legs. "I hate you, I hate you! I want to go home!"

Miss Smith grabbed him by the wrist and hauled him down the street in stony-faced silence. "Come along, Ada," she snapped, without looking back.

Jamie continued to sob. Snot ran down his chin. "I hate you!" he howled. "I hate you!"

"Trouble?" asked a calm voice. I looked up. It was the iron woman, the one who put us into her automobile, and by her side herself in miniature, an iron-faced girl. One of the bright girls in ribbons, who had served us tea.

To my surprise, Miss Smith rolled her eyes and shook her head, as though all Jamie's yelling hadn't bothered her a bit. "It's only a tantrum," she said. "He saw his friend leave."

The iron woman turned on Jamie. "Stop screaming," she said crisply. "Stop it this instant. You'll frighten the horses."

73

Jamie stopped. He looked around. "What horses?"

The iron woman said, "It's a figure of speech." To Miss Smith she said, "At least a dozen of them have gone back already. I've told their parents over and over that it isn't safe. London *will* be bombed. But it's no use. Those simple-minded women prefer their present comfort to the long-term safety of their children."

Simple-minded women. Simple like me. Maybe everyone was simple on my lane.

The iron woman eyed Jamie and me. "Yours are certainly looking better. A credit to you."

"Hardly," Miss Smith said. "All I did was put them in clean clothes and feed them." She rubbed stinky lotion on our impetigo too, but I noticed she didn't tell the iron woman that. Instead she said, hesitatingly, "Perhaps, if you have hand-me-downs—or if you know someone who does—I can't afford all they'll need for winter."

The iron lady pulled a clipboard out of her large handbag. She probably held a clipboard in her sleep. "Of course," she said, writing something down. "I'm organizing a used clothing collection in town. We don't expect you to be able to cover clothing out of the allowance. They were supposed to bring their own—

well, never mind. They should have come with more than they did. Obviously."

Her iron-faced daughter was staring at my bandaged foot. I leaned close and whispered, "It just happened yesterday. I got stepped on by our pony."

The girl's eyes narrowed. She whispered back, "That's an awful lie."

I said, "We have too got a pony."

She said, "It doesn't hurt that much when a pony steps on you. I've been stepped on dozens of times."

Well, she had me there. I didn't know what to say, so I stuck my tongue out at her. She bared her teeth in response, like a tiger. Cor.

Meanwhile Miss Smith was saying, "What allowance?"

It turned out she was getting paid for taking us in. *Nineteen shillings a week*! Nearly a whole pound! If she hadn't been rich before, she was now. I let out a deep breath. I could quit worrying over what my shoe had cost, and how much food we ate. Mam didn't earn anything like nineteen shillings a week. Jamie and I could eat all we wanted on nineteen shillings a week.

"I can't believe you didn't know that," the iron woman said. "Surely I explained—"

"Oh," Miss Smith said, with a little laugh, "I wasn't listening to a word you said."

As we continued down the street, Jamie subdued but still whimpering, I said, "That's three pounds sixteen shillings a month, miss. You could take in more of us and get rich."

Miss Smith scowled. "Thank God I'm not reduced to that."

Chapter 12

All this time, in secret, I'd been messing with Butter. What Miss Smith didn't know I was doing, she couldn't forbid.

The Tuesday that she stayed in bed I sat on him for the first time. I coaxed him to stand beside the stone wall, then climbed the wall—wobbling, without my crutches—and threw my bad leg across his back. I grabbed his mane and scrambled, and there I was, astride him. The smell of him rose up around me, and his coat felt warm and prickly against my legs.

He walked forward, his swinging steps moving my hips along with him. I held on to his mane for balance. I tried to steer him, but it didn't work, and before long he dropped his head to graze. I didn't mind. I sat on him most of that morning, until I grew hungry myself. Then I slid off him and went in to eat.

The next day my legs felt wobbly. All stretched out

in a new way. I didn't mind that either. It was nothing like as bad as walking.

The stables had a storeroom attached. It had been locked, but Jamie'd found the key under a rock near the door. Inside was all sorts of stuff I guessed had to do with Becky and her horses. I went looking for straps like I'd seen on the pony who raced our train, and found boxes full of leather pieces, some of them buckled together. I pulled them out and examined them.

If you pick up a bridle, which is the leather stuff that goes around the horse's head, by the wrong piece—by the noseband or the cheek piece, say, instead of the headstall—it doesn't look like anything that could go onto a horse. It just looks like a mess of leather. So at first I couldn't make sense of anything. Finally I found a sort of square thing on a shelf. It had pieces of paper covered in writing I couldn't read, and partway through had a drawing of a horse's head with the leather pieces fastened round. I studied it and the leather bits until I understood.

That afternoon, when I tried to bridle Butter, I must have been using tack that fit one of Becky's bigger horses. I got the headpiece over his ears, but the metal bit hung below his chin, and the part that should have wrapped around his head wrapped around his nostrils instead. He snorted and ran off, trailing the reins. It took me half the afternoon to catch him, and that was with Jamie's help.

On Thursday afternoon, when we got home from shopping, I tried a smaller bridle, and everything worked a treat. Butter came to me when I called. I fed him a piece of dried porridge from my pocket. I put the bridle on him, and it fit. (I didn't know the words then: bridle, bit, reins, cheek piece or headstall. But I know them now. And the thing with the pieces of paper and the picture of a bridled horse was a book. My first.)

Anyway, there stood Butter, bridled, and me, ready. When I climbed onto him he sighed, and went to put his head down to graze. I yanked on the reins, and he threw his head up, startled. That was better. I kicked him a bit, because I'd discovered this would make him move. He walked forward. I pulled on one side of the reins, and he turned. I pulled on both, and he stopped. It was all easy, I thought. I thumped him hard with my legs, to try to make him run. He threw his head down, bucked, and tossed me over his ears. I landed on my back in the grass.

Jamie ran to me. "Ada! Are you dead?"

I scrambled to my feet. "Not a bit."

I got back on and Butter tried it again. This time I

kept his head up, and he couldn't buck, not exactly, so he jumped sideways and got me off that way instead. I thunked my head on the ground and went dizzy for a moment.

"You can have a turn," I said to Jamie.

He shook his head. "I don't want one. I don't think he likes it."

I considered this. Butter might not like it right this moment, when he was used to eating all day long. But he'd like it later—later, when we were running, out in the open, soaring over stone walls. He'd like it then.

I liked it right away. Falling off didn't scare me. Learning to ride was like learning to walk. It hurt, but I kept on. If Miss Smith wondered why my new blouse was covered in grass stains, or how my new skirt got a rip near the hem, she never said a thing. She just sighed, as usual, and threw the shirt into the wash boiler and mended the rip with a shiny metal thing like a toothpick and a piece of thread.

"Why does she make that noise?" Jamie asked at night. He imitated Miss Smith's sigh. It wasn't a noise Mam ever made.

I shrugged. "She doesn't like us. She didn't want us, remember?" I tried not to make much work for her, so she wouldn't force the iron woman to take us back. I washed the dishes, and made Jamie dry. I went along with the baths and the hair-brushing, and I got Jamie to cooperate too. I even made him eat the strange food, though the only way to do that was by threatening him.

"How long do we have to stay here?" he asked.

"Dunno," I told him. "'Til the end of war, maybe, or 'til Mam comes to take us back."

"How long 'til the war ends?"

"Couple weeks, I guess. Maybe longer."

"I want to go home," Jamie said.

He said that all the time, and I was tired of hearing it. I turned on him. "Why?" I said, nearly spitting the word. I kept my voice low, but rage I didn't know I felt gushed out of me. "So you can do anything you want, and I can do nothing at all? So I can't boss you? So I can be shut up in a room?"

His round eyes filled with tears. "No," he said, in a whisper. "I don't care if you boss me. And she probably won't shut you up, now you've got crutches and all."

"Everybody thinks I'm nasty, back home. They think I'm some kind of monster."

"They don't," Jamie said, but he turned his face away. "They won't." He started crying in earnest, muffling his sobs in his pillow. "You've got crutches!" he said.

"Crutches don't change my foot!" I said. "It's still the same. It still hurts. I'm still the same!"

Jamie said, through sobs, "At home I know the words for things."

I knew what he meant. I knew how overwhelmed I felt sometimes, going into a shop full of things I'd never seen before. "There's nothing good at home," I said. "You were hungry. Remember?"

"No," said Jamie. "I wasn't ever hungry. I never was."

If he wasn't, it was only because I gave him most of the food. "I was," I said. "I was hungry, and I was alone, and I was trapped, and right now, no matter what, you have to do what I say. You have to stay here with me. I'm the person who keeps you safe."

Jamie's sobs slowed. He looked up at me, his brown eyes still brimming with tears. He rolled over onto his back and I pulled the sheet up to his chin. I patted his skinny shoulder. "Is this safe?" he asked.

It didn't feel safe. I never felt safe. "Yes," I said.

"You're lying. I know you are." Jamie flopped onto his side, turning his back to me. I lay flat on my back, breathing in the honeysuckle-scented air coming through the open windows. The curtains fluttered against the pale blue walls. I wasn't hungry. I fell asleep.

82

Chapter 13

The next time we went into town, we saw an enormous poster pasted to the brick wall near the train station. Jamie stopped to stare. "What's it say?" he asked.

Miss Smith read it aloud, tapping the words with her fingers as she went, "'Your courage, your cheerfulness, your resolution, will bring us victory.'"

"That's stupid," I said. "It sounds like we're doing all the work."

Miss Smith looked at me and laughed. "You're right," she said.

"It should be, 'our courage,'" I said. "*Our* courage, *our* cheerfulness, *our* resolution, will bring us victory."

"Absolutely," Miss Smith said. "I'll write the War Office and suggest a revision."

I couldn't tell if she meant it or not. I hated when I didn't understand her.

"I shouldn't underestimate you, should I?" Miss Smith went on.

How should I know? I scowled.

"Oh, come on, you cranky child," she said, touching my shoulder lightly. "You can help me pick out the veg."

Jamie was tugging on my arm. He pointed across the street, to Stephen White holding on to the arm of a very old man. Actually, I saw, it was the old man holding on to Stephen.

"A friend of yours?" Miss Smith asked.

"No," I said. "It's Billy's brother."

Miss Smith nodded. "You can go and say hello."

I felt funny doing it, but I did want to know why Stephen hadn't gone home with the rest of his family. I made my way across the street.

Stephen saw me. He stopped, and when he did the old man stopped too, turning odd milky eyes toward me.

Stephen gestured toward the crutches. "Good," he said. "You should have had those before."

I thought of him carrying me to the station, and my face went hot.

"Who's this?" barked the old man. "Who're you talking to? Somebody new?" He was looking straight at me, the old coot.

Stephen cleared his throat. "It's Ada," he said, "from our lane. Ada—"

The man said, crossly, "That's not the way you do a proper introduction. Haven't I taught you?"

"Yes, sir." Stephen took a deep breath. "Sir, may I present Miss Ada Smith, from London. Ada, this is Colonel Robert McPherson, British Army, retired. I live with him here."

The old man stuck one of his hands into the air. "And now you shake my hand, Miss Smith," he said. "If you're from the same place the boy's from, nobody's taught you proper manners either. You shake my hand, and you say, 'Nice to meet you, Colonel McPherson.'"

I touched his gnarled dry hand. He snatched my fingers and shook them up and down. "Say, 'Nice to meet you, Colonel McPherson,'" he ordered.

"Nice to meet you, Colonel McPherson," I said.

"And it's a pleasure to meet you, Miss Ada Smith. If you're a friend of Stephen's, you must come around for tea." He let go of my hand. I wiped it against my skirt, not because his hand had been dirty—it hadn't—but because touching a stranger seemed like such an odd thing to do.

Stephen was grinning, as though he found the whole exchange funny.

"How come you didn't go home?" I asked him.

"Oh," he said, cutting his eyes toward Colonel McPherson, "Mam thought it better if I stayed here for a while."

"No she didn't," I said. "She said—"

Stephen smacked me on the arm, hard. I glared at him. He nodded his head toward the old man, frowning. "What?" I asked.

"I'll talk to you later," Stephen said. "Later, okay?"

"Okay," I said, still puzzled.

Back on the other side of the street, Miss Smith and Jamie stood in front of a second poster. "This one's better," Jamie said.

"'Freedom is in peril,'" Miss Smith read. "'Defend it with all your might.'"

It was better. "What's 'might'?" I asked.

"I might have some tea," said Jamie.

"No—well, yes," Miss Smith said. "But in this case, it means strength. Force. Defend it with everything you've got."

"Freedom is in peril," Jamie shouted, running ahead. He waved his arms wildly. "Freedom is in peril, defend it with everything you've got!"

"What's 'freedom'?" I asked as Miss Smith and I followed.

"It's—hmmm. I'd say it's the right to make decisions about yourself," Miss Smith said. "About your life."

"Like, this morning we decided to come into town?"

"More like deciding that you want to be a—I don't know—a solicitor. When you grow up. Or, perhaps, a teacher. Or deciding that you'd like to live in Wales. Big decisions. If Germany invades, we'll probably still be able to go shopping, but we might not get to decide much else."

As usual, I mostly didn't understand her, but I was tired of trying. "Stephen White has to live with a grumpy old man," I said.

"I noticed," Miss Smith said. "I'm sorry to see the colonel looking so frail. He was one of Becky's foxhunting friends—one of the huntin', shootin', and fishin' sort. I didn't realize he was so old."

"He made me touch his hand." I shuddered.

"That's just manners," Miss Smith said.

"So he said."

Miss Smith grinned. I didn't know why. "Skeptical child," she said, making me frown even harder. She grabbed the end of my plait and swung it. "*Your* courage, *your* cheerfulness, *your* resolution"—she was saying it wrong. I scowled—"will bring *you* victory, my dear."

We'd reached the greengrocer's. Jamie waited for us, holding open the shop door. I flicked my plait away from Miss Smith. I wasn't going to ask what any more words meant, I was so tired of words, but Miss Smith looked at me and answered my question anyway. "Victory," she said, "means peace."

Chapter 14

A few days later the teacher who'd been with us on the train came by the house to say that school was starting. The village didn't have an empty building big enough to hold the evacuated children, so the evacuees had to share the village school. The regular village students would attend with their regular teachers from eight until noon, and then the evacuees and the evacuated teachers would go from one in the afternoon until five.

The teacher gave Miss Smith directions to the school. "We'll see you Monday afternoon," she said to Jamie as she got up to leave.

We'd all four been sitting in the main room of Miss Smith's house, on the squishy purple chairs and sofa. Miss Smith had made tea. Now she smiled quizzically at the teacher and said, "Ada too, of course."

I don't know how I looked, but Jamie's and the teacher's mouths fell open. The teacher's mouth closed first. "Ada's not on our list," she said. "I told you that when I gave you their mother's address. We've only got Jamie down."

Jamie said, "Ada's not allowed to go outside."

I said fiercely, "That's rubbish, it was only ever in London and you know it."

"But not *school*," said Jamie.

I'd never been. Never thought about going. But why not? I could get there on my crutches, it wasn't that far.

Miss Smith argued that lists didn't matter. Surely the lists weren't accurate, and besides, many of the children had already gone back to London. There had to be room for me.

"Room, yes," the teacher said slowly, "but is it appropriate?" She stood and took a book off one of Miss Smith's shelves. "Here," she said, holding it open and out to me, "read a bit of that."

I looked at the page. The rows of marks blurred and swam before my eyes. I looked up. The teacher nodded. Miss Smith came over and put her arm around me. I tried to pull away, but Miss Smith held on.

"You see," the teacher said softly, "she isn't educable."

I didn't know what educable meant. I didn't know if I was educable or not.

"She simply hasn't been taught," Miss Smith said. "She's far from stupid. She deserves a chance."

The teacher shook her head. "It wouldn't be fair to the others."

The door clicked softly as she left. Miss Smith grabbed my shoulders with both hands. "Don't cry," she said. "Don't cry, she isn't right, I know you can learn. Don't cry."

Why would I cry? I never cried. But when I shook myself free of Miss Smith's grasp, tears shook loose from my eyes and slid down my cheeks. Why would I cry? I wanted to hit something, or throw something, or scream. I wanted to gallop on Butter and never stop. I wanted to run, but I couldn't run, not with my twisted, ugly, horrible foot. I buried my head in one of the fancy pillows on the sofa, and then I couldn't help it, I did cry.

I was so tired of being alone.

Miss Smith sat down on the sofa beside me. She put her hand on my back. I squirmed away. "Don't worry," she said, almost like she cared about me. "They're wrong. We'll find another way.

"I know you aren't stupid," she continued. "Stupid people couldn't take care of their brother the way you do. Stupid people aren't half as brave as you. They're not half as strong."

Stupid. Simple. Educable. Thoughtful. All just words. I was so tired of meaningless words.

That night, after our baths, Miss Smith came to the doorway of our bedroom before we fell asleep. She hesitated. "I've brought something," she said. "This was my favorite book when I was a little girl. My father used to read it to me at bedtime. I thought I'd start reading it to you."

I turned my head away. More words. Jamie asked, "Why, miss?"

"I wish you'd quit calling me *miss*," she said, pulling the chair close to Jamie's side of the bed. "My name is Susan. You should call me that. I'm reading to you because I think you'll enjoy it."

Jamie said, "Why would we enjoy it?"

Miss Smith didn't answer. She said, "This book is called *The Swiss Family Robinson*. Listen." She cleared her throat and began. "'For many days we had been tempest-tossed. Six times darkness closed over a wild and terrific scene . . .'"

I buried my head deeper into my pillow. The drone of her voice sounded like a fly buzzing against a window. I fell asleep.

In the morning, though, those first words stuck in my head until I couldn't stand it anymore. "Miss?"

I said at breakfast. "What's 'tempest-tossed'?"

Miss Smith looked at me over her mug of tea. "Caught in a storm," she said. "Wind and rain and lightning, and if you're in a boat, at sea, you get tossed from side to side. You're all thrown about, because of the storm."

I looked at Jamie. "That's us," I said. "All thrown about. We're tempest-tossed." He nodded.

I turned back to Miss Smith. "What's 'educable'?"

She cleared her throat. "Able to be educated," she said. "Able to learn. You are plenty able to learn, Ada. You are educable. I know you are. That teacher is wrong."

A plane zoomed overhead. Jamie jumped up. We heard and saw planes all the time now, because of the airfield, but Jamie never tired of watching them. I got up to go out too.

"Ada," Miss Smith said, "if you like, this morning I'll start to teach you to read."

I edged away. "No, thank you," I said, using the manners she taught me. "I want to go look at the planes."

She shook her head. "That's not true."

"I want to talk to Butter."

Miss Smith leaned forward. "You're perfectly capable of learning. You mustn't listen to people who don't know you. Listen to what you know, yourself."

What I knew, I'd learned looking out a single window. I knew nothing. Words she used—*capable, tempest-tossed.* Even little words, *sea.* What was a sea? Boats came down the River Thames. Was a sea the same as a river? I knew nothing, nothing at all.

"I need to see the pony," I said.

She sighed. "Suit yourself," she said, and turned away.

I'd found a brush in the storage room and I used it all over Butter's yellow coat. Dust and loose hair flew up. I could tell he liked it. "Good, isn't it?" I asked him. "Gets the itches out."

My skin didn't itch the way it used to. The stinky lotion cleared up the rough patches on my skin, and my head felt better now that Miss Smith brushed my hair for me every morning. She braided it for me into a single plait down my back, so it stayed neater, out of my way in the wind, and wasn't as tangled at night. She brushed me the way I brushed Butter, which was odd no matter how I thought about it.

"Look," Jamie cried, pointing to the sky. "It's a different one!" He ran across the pasture, trying to get a better view of the plane.

I rode Butter twice around the field before he got me off.

———

At lunch Miss Smith said she would walk Jamie to school for the first day. "You'll be all right by yourself, Ada?" she asked. "Or you could come."

I shook my head. I wasn't going near the school. And that turned out to be lucky. The minute Miss Smith left with Jamie I climbed back onto Butter, and so I was there when the strange horse jumped into our field.

Chapter 15

It happened like this. I was walking Butter in circles, practicing making him turn. I heard a sound like hoof beats coming from the road, and I stopped to look, but couldn't yet see anything through the trees. A plane took off from the airfield and screamed straight over our heads just as a horse and rider came into view. Butter didn't mind the plane—he saw dozens of planes take off every day now—but the other horse, a big brown one, wheeled in fright. His rider pulled the reins sharply to keep him from bolting, but he wheeled again, and then jumped forward, off the road and onto the verge, nearly chesting the stone wall into our field. The rider bounced loose in the saddle, and the horse, frantic, made a sudden leap up and over the wall. The rider tumbled sideways and disappeared.

The strange horse galloped straight for Butter, reins flying, loose stirrups walloping his sides. Butter spooked and spun, tossing me, and together both horses ran to the far side of the field. They galloped about for a bit, the idiots, but I wasn't paying attention to them. I ran for the fallen rider as fast as my bad foot would let me. I'd recognized her: the little iron-faced girl. The one who'd called me out.

She lay facedown in the muddy weeds on the verge. I scrambled over the wall just as she, blinking, rolled herself over. She opened her eyes and let out a string of curses that would have been at home in my lane, let alone the dockyards. She ended with, "I hate that stupid bloody horse."

Bloody is not something Miss Smith let Jamie or me say. It was a swear word, a bad one.

"I hate him," she repeated, looking at me.

"Are you much hurt?"

She started to sit up, then fell back, nodding. "Dizzy," she said. "And my shoulder hurts something awful. Bet I broke my collarbone." She touched a place below her neck, and winced. "My mother broke hers last year, hunting. Easy to do. Where's the wretched horse?"

I looked over the wall. "Grazing next to the pony. Acts like nothing's wrong."

She pulled herself slowly to a sitting position. "He would. I hate him. He belongs to my brother." She started to stand, gave a small cry, and sat back down with a thump. Her skin went pale, then an interesting shade of gray.

"Better stay still," I told her. I went to fetch the horse. His front foot was tangled in the reins, but otherwise he seemed fine, and he stood politely while I untangled him. He was bigger than Butter, and far more handsome—beautiful shiny coat, long elegant legs. He sniffed my hands the way Butter often did. "No treats," I told him.

I started to walk him back to the girl, but honestly, my foot hurt, and also the horse was so pretty. I pulled the reins over his head, put my good foot into the left stirrup, and hauled myself aboard.

The saddle felt snug and comfortable after the loose sliding expanse of Butter's bare back. I couldn't put my bad foot into a stirrup, but I liked the feel of the stirrup on my good foot. I gathered the reins up, and the horse delicately arched his neck.

I thumped him with my heels, and he nearly bolted. My mistake. Clearly the horse responded to much softer signals than Butter. I pulled him back, and used my legs very gently. He walked forward, a fine, long-striding, loopy sort of walk.

Now the girl was standing, hanging on to the wall. She called, "Take him around by the gate."

I had a better idea. The horse had jumped in; it

could jump out. I kicked him forward. He took a few enormously bouncy strides, then settled into a nice smooth run. *Oh,* I thought, my breath catching in my throat. *This was what it felt like to move fast without pain.* I pulled on the reins and aimed the horse straight for the wall. He never hesitated—up and over in one smooth bound. *Flying.* I held on to his mane with both hands and flew with him. We landed together on the other side. I laughed out loud.

"Show-off," the girl said, but she was laughing too. "Lucky you there isn't another airplane."

"Lucky me," I said. "Can you ride him now?"

She moved her right arm experimentally, and winced. "I'll never be able to hold him," she said. "Not one-handed. And my head hurts terribly. Can I get up behind you?"

I scooched forward. The saddle was plenty big. I took my foot out of the stirrup and helped pull her onto the horse. "You can have the foot things," I said.

She put her good arm around my waist. "They're called stirrups," she said, slipping her feet into them. "Just go back the way I came from. And walk, please. My head feels like it's smashed in two. A trot would be the end of me."

Her name was Margaret. Her mother was the head of the Women's Volunteer Service, which was why she was in charge of the evacuees. "But that's not all," Margaret said. "She does war work all the time. She's trying to stay busy so she doesn't have time to worry about Jonathan. She wants to win the war herself before he's part of the fighting." Jonathan, Margaret's brother, was learning to fly planes at a different airfield, far from here. He'd left Oxford to do it, Margaret said.

"You talk like our evacuees," she said. "The same funny accent."

I said, "You talk funny to me."

She laughed. "I guess. But you can ride, and our evacuees, the ones staying with us, I mean, are all terrified of horses. Where'd you learn to ride in London?"

"Didn't. Just teaching myself here."

"Well, you're pretty good."

"On a posh horse like this one, anyone would be," I said. "Our pony has me off half a dozen times a day."

"Ponies are snakes," she replied. "Sneaky devils. You should see what mine gets up to."

It turned out the horse we were riding was her brother's hunter, and her mother was making her keep it exercised. "Just until I leave for school," she said. "Which should have been last week, only they're moving the school, evacuating it, I suppose, so we're starting late. And I hate this horse, I do, and he hates me. Goes like a lamb for anybody else. Mum won't believe me, and he's worse when he's by himself, and he won't pony with my mare, so I'm stuck fighting him alone for an hour a day. All the stable lads have run off to join up and Grimes is overworked and there's nobody to go with me."

All this talk—which I only half understood—seemed to suddenly exhaust her. She sagged against my shoulder. "You're all right?" I asked.

"Not really," she said. "I feel sick."

The horse swung authoritatively around a corner. I hoped he knew where he was going. He seemed to, and anyway, Margaret wasn't telling me anything different.

She swayed suddenly. I wished I was behind her, so I could hold her steady. "Maggie?" I said. There was a Margaret on our lane and everyone called her Maggie. "Maggie, hang on."

I pulled her hand farther around my waist. She leaned her head between my shoulder blades, muttering to herself. I worked hard to keep the horse steady but walking fast. I didn't know how far we had to go.

"M'mother likes Jonathan better than me," Maggie said, more loudly. "She doesn't really like girls. She'll do anything for him, but she's always cross with me."

"My mam likes my brother better too," I said. "She hates me, because of my foot."

I could feel her lean over to look at my bad foot. I was glad that it was bandaged. She swayed, off balance. "Careful," I said.

"Mmm," she said.

"A brewer's cart ran over it," I said.

"Oh," Maggie said. "Well, that's a silly reason to hate you."

The horse clomped on. Maggie's head bounced against my shoulder. "It wasn't a brewer's cart," I said, after a pause. "It's a clubfoot." That word the doctor had used.

"Oh, clubfoot." Her voice slurred. "I've heard of that. We had a foal born with a clubfoot."

The horse turned again, down a long gravel drive planted on both sides with straight rows of trees. He stepped faster now, swinging his head. Maggie groaned. "I'm going to be sick," she said.

"Not on the horse," I said.

"Mmm," she said, and was, but she leaned over far enough that most of the sick missed the saddle. Then she nearly fell off. I grabbed her. The horse swung his head impatiently.

"He's always happier going home," Maggie murmured. "Rotten bugger."

"What's a foal?" I asked.

"What? Oh—a baby horse. We had a horse born with a clubfoot. That's what Grimes called it." She swayed again. "I feel awful."

I tried to imagine a little horse with a twisted hoof. Butter's hooves were long and curling, but they didn't twist. What would a horse do if it couldn't walk? No crutches for horses. Were there?

"Did it die, then?" I asked.

"What? Oh, the horse. The clubfoot horse. No. Grimes fixed it. Grimes and the farrier."

The trees opened up and in front of us was a huge stone building, big like I imagined the dock warehouses must be. Big like the London train station. It couldn't be right. Whatever the place was, it wasn't a house.

The horse shook his head at my attempts to rein him in. Instead of heading straight for the massive building, he went around to the side, to what even I could recognize was a stable.

An elderly man came forward at a sort of running limp. Grimes, I thought. "What's happened?" he asked.

"Our Maggie's hurt," I told him. She tumbled sideways into his arms. He staggered, but held on to her. "She fell off an' smacked her head," I said. "Hurt her shoulder too."

Grimes nodded. "Can you stay with the horse a moment? I'll get her to the house."

"Of course," I said, trying make my voice sound like Maggie's. *Grimes fixed a horse with a clubfoot. Fixed a clubfoot. How?*

He carried Maggie away. I slid off the horse—a very long way to the ground—and looked around. There were stalls just like the closed-up ones at Miss Smith's house, only more of them, and fancier, and mostly occupied. Horses looked over the open tops of the stalls' half-doors, their ears pricked with interest. Some of them made little murmuring sounds.

I led Maggie's brother's horse into an empty stall. The horse thrust his head into a water bucket and then into a pile of hay. I got the saddle off him—not hard, just buckles under the flap bits—and slung it over the door, then got the bridle off. I shut the horse in the stall and carried the tack and bridle to their storeroom, which I found without any trouble. One row of racks held saddles, and another bridles, and I put the kit I held into the empty spaces. I wandered around looking at the other horses until Grimes returned.

"Thank you," he said. "She's in bed now, and m'lady has phoned for the doctor. Don't think there's anything more we can do. She doesn't know where she is right now. You get that sometimes, with a smack on the head."

"She seemed all right at first," I said. "She got worse as we were going."

"I'm not surprised." He pointed to my foot. "What happened? You get hurt too?"

I looked down. A small bloodstain was seeping through the bandage. "Oh," I said. "It does that, sometimes. When I don't have my crutches." I hesitated, then added, "It's a clubfoot."

Grimes didn't offer to fix it. He nodded and said, "I'll give you a ride home in the car, then."

Grimes took me home very nicely. He thanked me for helping "Miss Margaret." I told him I was glad to, especially since it meant I got to ride such a big fancy horse. He laughed a bit at that, and patted my hand, which was odd but okay with me. I felt completely happy as I went through the front door. I was totally unprepared for Miss Smith's rage.

Chapter 16

She came at me like a small yellow-haired witch, eyes blazing. "Where have you BEEN?" she shouted. "I've nearly gone to the police. Pony's in the field with a bridle on, you're nowhere. *It's almost four o'clock.* What on earth were you thinking?"

She came toward me. I ducked, my arms around my head. "I'm not going to hit you!" she roared. "Though I feel like it. You half deserve a whipping, making me worry like that."

Worry? Worry the way I worried over Jamie, in London? I dropped my hands to my lap—I'd sat down in one of the purple chairs—and stared at her, perplexed.

"I know you don't like strangers," she said, more quietly. "I couldn't imagine a reason you'd go into town. I didn't think you'd go to the airfield, but I went there to ask anyway, and they hadn't seen you. Here it's the first time I left you alone—I couldn't imagine what could go wrong. I didn't have any idea where you could be."

"I thought I was allowed to go outside," I said. My foot hurt, worse than it had for days. I hadn't walked so far without my crutches since I'd first come here. I had a scratch down my arm too, that had left a thin trail of blood.

"You can't leave without telling me," Miss Smith said. She looked less angry, but still unpredictable. "You've got to let me know where you go."

How could I have done that? "I had to help Maggie," I said. I told her about the horse, how the plane spooked it, how Maggie fell.

Miss Smith snorted. "Maggie? Who's Maggie?"

I tried to explain. I told about the big horse, and the house and stables.

"The Honorable Margaret Thorton?" Miss Smith asked, her eyes widening. "Lady Thorton's daughter?"

I shrugged. "I suppose. She's got a brother called Jonathan."

"The girl we met with Lady Thorton, last week in the market?"

I nodded.

Miss Smith sat down in the other chair. "The whole story," she demanded.

I told the whole story, except for the part where Maggie said bad words. Miss Smith straightened up. Her face looked grim. "So," she said. "You rode Jonathan Thorton's prize hunter double with Miss Margaret, back to her home?"

"Yes," I said.

"I don't believe you," Miss Smith said.

I didn't know what to say. I told lies, of course I did. But I wouldn't lie about this. I'd been helpful. I'd done a good job, getting Maggie and the horse home. Grimes had said so. He'd tipped his cap to me, when I got out of the car.

"I wouldn't know where she lived," I said, "if it wasn't true."

"Oh, I believe you saw the house," Miss Smith said bitterly. "I believe Miss Margaret rode by, and you saw them and followed them. Look at the state you're in—foot bleeding again and everything. I believe you saw Margaret, the horse, and the house. I just don't believe any of the rest of it."

My mouth opened, then shut. I didn't know what to say.

"Go to your room," Miss Smith said. "Wash yourself off in the bathroom, then go to your room and stay there. I don't want to see you again today. I'll send Jamie up with some supper once he's home."

Hours later Jamie came up with a plate for me. "How was school?" I asked.

"I hate it," he said, his eyes dark. "I'm never going back."

Later still Miss Smith came up with her horrible book. She sat down on the chair on Jamie's side of the bed, and she opened the book without looking at me. I ignored her too. Jamie snugged himself into the blankets. "What happens next?" he asked, as though the book was something he cared about.

"You'll see," Miss Smith said, smiling at him. She opened the book and started to read.

Next morning at breakfast Jamie said again he wasn't going back to school. "Of course you are," Miss Smith said. "You want to learn to read. Then you can read *Swiss Family Robinson* all by yourself."

Jamie looked up at her through his eyelashes. "I'd rather you read it to me," he said sweetly. Miss Smith smiled at him, and the thought ran through me that I hated them both.

Out in the field that afternoon, I couldn't make Butter go faster than a walk. I tried and tried. I kicked and squeezed with my legs. I even snapped a branch off a tree and smacked Butter's side with it. He lurched forward for a few stumbling steps, but dropped back almost immediately to his usual shuffle. It wasn't his fault that he wasn't elegant like Jonathan's horse, but I was sure he could do better if he tried.

Miss Smith opened the back door. "Ada," she called, "come here, please."

Right. I pretended I hadn't heard, and turned Butter so our backsides faced her.

"Ada," she called again, "you've got a visitor."

Maggie? Grimes? *Mam?* I slid off Butter, pulled the bridle off his head—I wasn't going to get chewed out for leaving it on him again—hobbled to my crutches leaning against the wall, and went into the house as quickly as I could.

The visitor was Lady Thorton. She was smiling. Her face looked different when she smiled.

"She's come to thank you," Miss Smith said, in an oddly stiff voice.

I stood in the doorway, staring at them, hiding my right foot behind my left. To break the silence I said, "How is she? Maggie, I mean."

Lady Thorton—Maggie's mum—patted the empty spot on the sofa beside her. I sat down on it, folded my hands, and slid my right foot behind my left.

"She's much better today, thank you," Lady Thorton said. "She woke with a headache, but she knows where and who she is."

"She seemed all right when she first came off," I said. "She got worse as we went on."

Lady Thorton nodded. "Head injuries can be like that. She tells me she doesn't remember much of what happened. She remembers you were there, but that's about all. Grimes in the stable told me how you brought her home."

I glanced at Miss Smith. Her face still looked stiff, like it was made from cardboard. I said, nodding toward her, "She didn't believe me, that I rode that horse an' all."

Lady Thorton opened a box near her feet. "I might not have believed it myself without a witness. That's not an easy horse."

"He likes me." It slipped out before I thought, but I realized it was true. Jonathan's horse did like me.

Now Lady Thorton's face looked strained. "Then you're the third person that animal has ever actually liked, after Grimes and my son." She shook her head, once, sharply, and her face took on its official look. The iron-face look. "I brought over some clothing for you and your brother. Your brother's is from an assortment of village families. Yours is mostly from my daughter. Things she's outgrown. Here."

She laid a pair of yellow pants and a pair of ankle boots across my lap. I stared at them. The pants were made of a thick, tough fabric, with legs that ballooned wide at the top, then narrowed and buttoned below the knee. I recognized them: Maggie had worn a pair just like them the day before. "For riding," I said. I'd never worn pants before. It would be easier, on Butter.

Lady Thorton nodded. "Yes. I'm sure Miss Smith's helping you, but I didn't think she'd be able to find you the proper clothes."

Miss Smith said, very softly, "I haven't helped her. She's done it on her own."

Lady Thorton looked me up and down. "Margaret needs to stay in bed a few days. She won't be able to ride again before she leaves for school. But if you have questions about horses, you can always go to our stables and ask Grimes. I know he'll help you."

I noticed she wasn't offering to help me herself. I said, "Butter doesn't want to go fast. I don't know how to make him."

She gave a little laugh, and tapped my knee as she stood. "Persistence," she said. "Ponies are stubborn until they know who's boss. Enjoy the new things."

Miss Smith saw her out. When she came back in,

she sat down in Lady Thorton's place. "I'm sorry," she said, after a moment's pause. "I didn't mean to call you a liar."

Sure she did. I shrugged. "I am one."

"I know." She began to empty the rest of the box of clothes. Shorts for Jamie, sweaters, shirts. Then she straightened. "No," she said. "That's wrong, I don't know that. We both know you sometimes tell lies, but I can't say that it makes you a liar. Do you understand what I mean?"

Blouses, sweaters, skirts for me. A red dress with lace on the cuffs. Coats for winter.

I touched the girl's coat. Maggie's coat. "Will I still be here in winter?"

"I don't know," Miss Smith said. "Do you understand what I just said? The difference between lying and being a liar?"

I shrugged. Miss Smith persisted. "If you have to tell lies, or you think you have to, to keep yourself safe—I don't think that makes you a liar. Liars tell lies when they don't need to, to make themselves look special or important. That's what I thought you were doing yesterday. I was wrong."

I didn't want to talk about it. "Why is Maggie going away for school?" I asked instead. "Why doesn't she go to school where Jamie does?"

"Rich people educate their children at boarding schools," Miss Smith replied. "Margaret won't have to leave school at fourteen to work, like most children do. She'll stay at school until she's sixteen or seventeen. If the war's over by then she'll probably go to finishing school. She might even go to university."

"What kind of school did you go to?" I asked.

"A boarding school," she said. "Not because my family was rich—they weren't. I was bright and my father is a clergyman, and some schools offer scholarships to the bright daughters of clergymen."

"What's a clergyman?"

"You know—a vicar. A man who runs a church."

The "you know" kept me from asking more. "Churches are where the bells are."

"Yes," said Miss Smith. "Only they aren't going to be allowed to ring the bells anymore. Only in case of invasion, to warn us."

I smoothed the pants with my hand. Tomorrow I'd wear them. The left boot too.

"Ada?" Miss Smith said. "I wish I'd believed you."

I darted a quick glance at her and shrugged again.

Chapter 17

When Jamie came home it was obvious he'd been crying, but he wouldn't say why. He wet the bed in the night and woke up miserable. Outside, gray clouds were spitting rain. "I can't go to school in the rain," Jamie said.

"Of course you can," Miss Smith replied. She looked awful, her hair every which way and great dark circles under her eyes. She held her mug of tea in both hands and stared into it.

"I ain't going," Jamie said.

"Don't start with me," Miss Smith replied.

We sat down to breakfast and a plane blew up at the airfield.

It crashed, I guess. It didn't blow up in the air, it blew up because it slammed into the ground. The gas tank ruptured. We learned that later. It sounded like a bomb exploding—like a bomb in Butter's pasture. We all jumped up, knocking over dishes and chairs. I ran toward the door, toward Butter, but Miss Smith grabbed me and Jamie and pushed us beneath the table. After a moment when nothing else happened she got up and looked out the window. "Oh," she said, "it's an airplane."

Under billows of black smoke across the road, we could see orange flames and twisted pieces of metal. Jamie cried out, and would have run to the airfield, but Miss Smith held him back. "No civilians," she said. "No civilians, not now. See? They're getting the fire out." We could see servicemen and women, tiny in the distance, working frantically all around the burning plane.

"Who was the pilot?" Jamie asked. "Who was the crew?"

"We don't know them," Miss Smith said, stroking his hair.

"I knew them," Jamie said.

I wasn't sure how Jamie could know them—there was a big fence around the airfield now, and he knew he wasn't allowed there, though of course that wouldn't really stop him—but I didn't say anything. I wasn't going to call him a liar, not over a dead airman.

"I wonder what kind of plane it was," Miss Smith said.

"A Lysander," Jamie said. "A transport plane. It

could have had ten people on board." We looked at him. He said, "That's what it sounded like. Before the crash."

I was so used to the sound of planes, I never paid attention to them anymore. The different kinds of planes didn't sound different to me.

Jamie leaned into Miss Smith's arms. She held him tight, rocking him softly back and forth. I stood still, absorbing what I was seeing: Jamie turning for comfort to someone other than me.

We ran into Lady Thorton in the village when we were shopping later that week, and she told us that Maggie—she called her Margaret, of course—had gone off to her school, and wouldn't be home until Christmas. I was sorry not to see her again. I wanted to talk to her when she hadn't just been hit on the head. I wanted to know if she'd still like me when she wasn't woozy.

Jamie kept hating school. He skipped twice, and after that the teacher wrote Miss Smith a note, and Miss Smith started to walk him to school every afternoon. Once he was inside the building, he was trapped.

I knew how it felt to be trapped. I'd been trapped all summer in our flat. I'll been trapped all my life in our flat. But I couldn't understand why Jamie hated school. Most of the kids from our neighborhood back home were there, including all of Jamie's friends except Billy White. They had breaks where they got to run and play in the school yard. Plus, pretty soon he'd be able to write and read, and then Miss Smith wouldn't have to read us *Swiss Family Robinson* at night anymore. Jamie could read it to himself.

"I don't want to talk about it," he said, when we asked him. "I'm sorry," he said, when he wet the bed, which he did every night now. "I want to go home," he told me.

"You'd miss Miss Smith," I said nastily.

"I wouldn't," he said. "I'd have Mam."

I could imagine Mam might have softened toward us, or at least toward Jamie. She probably missed us at least a little.

"They have school at home too," I said.

He shrugged. "Mam won't make me go." I knew this was probably true.

Meanwhile Miss Smith was in a fit because Mam hadn't responded to any of her letters. She asked me, "Does your mother know how to read?"

I shrugged. How would I know?

"Surely there's a social worker—a priest—someone who could read it to her, and write out her reply?"

Probably there was, but Mam would never ask them. "Why's it matter?" I asked. So long as Mam knew where we were, and could come get us when she decided to. "Do you want her to come take us home?"

Miss Smith gave me a strange look. "I do not. You know why it matters."

I didn't.

Sometimes I was so angry about everything I didn't know.

Miss Smith bought acres of black material for the blackout. We'd been under blackout regulations since the first day of evacuation, before the war even began. It meant that nobody, no houses, buildings, shops, or even things like buses or cars, was supposed to show any sort of light outside after the sun went down. That way if the Germans came to bomb at night, they wouldn't be able to see where any of the cities or villages were. It was harder to hit a dark place than a lit one.

For the first month Miss Smith hadn't bothered covering the windows—she just didn't put any lights on at night. Jamie and I went to bed before the sun went down, so we didn't care, and Miss Smith could sit and brood in a dark room as easily as in a bright one.

But now the sun was setting earlier, so Miss Smith made blackout curtains for the upstairs windows, and fabric stretched over frames for the windows downstairs.

We stayed up late one Saturday, putting all the blackout up, then turning on all the lights inside. Jamie and I walked around the house outside, looking for any chinks of light, and yelling to Miss Smith when we saw one. She adjusted the curtains until the chinks were gone.

Afterward she made us hot cocoa. "Very good," she said. "I'm sure we'll get used to having the house this dark." She looked almost happy, almost cheerful for a change.

I wondered what it would be like if Jamie and I really were stuck here all winter. I hated winter in the flat, so cold. Miss Smith had a fireplace in the main room. She could burn coal.

"I haven't had my sewing machine out since Becky died," she continued. "It felt good to be making something, even if it was only those awful curtains. I suppose I might run up a few things for the two of you."

Miss Smith had made us try on all the clothes Lady Thorton brought, and give back whatever didn't fit.

She'd also thrown away the clothes we'd come from London in. Still, I had three blouses, two skirts, two sweaters, a dress, a coat, and a pair of riding pants: more clothes than I'd owned in my lifetime. I couldn't imagine needing anything else. "Dressing gowns," Miss Smith said, as though reading my mind. "For winter. Something warm you can ride in. Perhaps something pretty? The red dress is very nice, but it's not the best color for you." She looked at me in a way that gave me the feeling of being a fish on a slab. "Blue, perhaps. Or a nice bottle green. Green's a good color with your complexion. Velvet? I loved the velvet dress I had as a girl."

"I hate velvet," I said.

She laughed. "You wouldn't know velvet if your underwear was made from it," she said. "Ada, that's a fib. Why?"

I said, "I don't want you making me things."

Her smile faded. "Why not?"

I shrugged. I had more than I needed. More than I felt comfortable with, really. I was still the girl I'd seen in the train station mirror, still the feeble-minded girl stuck behind a window. The simple one. I was okay with wearing Maggie's castoffs, but I knew my limits.

Jamie leaned forward. "Will you make me a velvet?" he asked.

Miss Smith's smile returned. "I will not," she said. "I'll make you something stout and manly."

Jamie nodded. "Like in the book," he said.

In the book, that stupid Swiss Family Robinson was all the time making and finding things. It was like magic, it was, how the father would think it was a shame they didn't have any wheat for bread, and next thing they'd stumble onto a whole wheatfield, or a wild pig would run out of the forest just when they got a hankering for bacon. They'd build a mill to grind the wheat to flour, and a smokehouse for the pork, out of nails and wood they just happened to have on hand. Jamie loved it; he begged for more of the story every night. I was tired of those idiots living on an island with everything they could ever want. I didn't care if I never heard another word.

"You won't have time to make us anything," I said. "We won't be here that long."

Miss Smith paused. "The war doesn't seem to be moving very quickly," she said.

"Right." More and more of the evacuated children had gone back to London, but not us. Not yet. "You'll be glad to get rid of us," I said. "You didn't want us in the first place."

Miss Smith sighed. "Ada, can't we have a happy night? Can't we drink cocoa and be happy together? I know I said I didn't want evacuees, but I've explained, it wasn't anything to do with you. I didn't *not* choose you."

Everyone else did. I put my mug down. "I hate cocoa," I said, and went to bed.

It was Miss Smith, not me, who saw the welt on Jamie's wrist.

Chapter 18

We were having dinner. Jamie reached across the table for another piece of bread and Miss Smith grabbed his arm. "What's that?" she asked.

When she pushed his sleeve back I saw the deep red mark on Jamie's wrist. It reminded me of when I'd tied him up in our flat, only worse: His skin had been rubbed away until it bled. It looked awful.

Jamie snatched his arm back. "Nothin'," he said, pushing his cuff back down.

"That's not nothing," Miss Smith said. "What happened?"

He wouldn't say.

"Did somebody hurt you?" I asked. "Somebody tie you up? Some boy at school?"

Jamie looked at his plate. He shrugged.

"Oh, honestly," Miss Smith said. "Speak up! You can't let people bully you. Tell us what's wrong so we can help you."

He wouldn't talk, not then nor later to me in the bed. "You've got to tell me," I coaxed. "I take care of you, remember?"

He wouldn't tell.

At lunch the next day Miss Smith surprised me by saying, "Ada, would you like to come with me to take Jamie to school? We might do a bit of shopping on the way home." I was worried enough about Jamie that I nodded, even though I suspected her of plans involving velvet.

Miss Smith marched Jamie into the school building the way I supposed she always did. I stayed outside. "We'll go get a cup of tea," she said, when she returned, "and come back in half an hour."

We went to a tea shop, which was a place full of tables where you could buy things to eat and drink. Like a pub, only without beer, and cleaner.

"Miss," I whispered, taking my seat, "why are there blankets on the tables?"

"They're called tablecloths," Miss Smith whispered back. "They're to make the tables look nice."

Huh, I thought. Imagine dressing up tables. Imagine wasting cloth to dress up tables.

A lady came over and Miss Smith asked for scones and a pot of tea. I remembered to put my napkin on my lap and to say thank you to the lady when she brought the tea, and the lady smiled and said, "What nice manners! She's an evacuee?"

I didn't know how the lady could tell, and I didn't like it that she could. Miss Smith said, "It's your accent, you talk different from us country people."

I talked different from posh people is what she meant. I knew I did, and I didn't like it, either. I was trying the best I could to sound like I fit in.

When we finished our tea we went back to the school. Miss Smith walked right into the building without saying anything. She marched down the hall and threw open the first classroom door. She didn't knock. I caught up to her just as she sucked in her breath. I looked inside and saw what she saw.

The whole class, including Jamie, was working at their desks with pencils and paper. Jamie's left hand was tied to his chair.

It was tied tight even though he already had a bloody welt on his wrist.

When I'd tied him up, at least I had let him go right away.

Miss Smith said, "What is the meaning of this?" in a voice that made some of the little girls jump. Jamie saw us. His face flooded red.

Miss Smith went to him and untied his arm. Jamie ducked. He ducked like he expected her to hit him, the way I ducked sometimes. Miss Smith said, "Jamie, I'm so sorry, I should have come sooner," and put her arms around him. Jamie leaned against her. He started to sob.

All this time I'd stood frozen in the doorway. Most of the students sat frozen at their desks. The only sounds were Jamie crying and Miss Smith murmuring words I couldn't quite understand.

The teacher unfroze herself with a jerk. She advanced on Miss Smith, eyes blazing. "I'll thank you not to interfere!" she said. "Every time my back's turned he's using that hand of his. I won't have it! I wouldn't have to tie him if he'd obey me."

Miss Smith held her ground. Her eyes glittered. "Why shouldn't he use that hand?"

The teacher gasped. I didn't recognize her, though I supposed she'd been on our train. She was an older woman with gray hair braided around her head, and round wire eyeglasses and a skirt that was too tight. When she gasped, her mouth went perfectly round, like her glasses. She looked like a fish. "It's his *left* hand," she said. "Everyone knows that's the mark of the devil. He wants to write with his left hand, not his right. I'm training him up the way he's supposed to be."

"I never heard such rubbish," snapped Miss Smith. "He's left-handed, that's all."

"It's the mark of the devil," insisted the teacher.

Miss Smith took a deep breath. "When I was at Oxford," she said, "my professor of Divinity, Dr. Henry Leighton Goudge, was left-handed. It is *not* the mark of the devil. Dr. Goudge told me himself that fear of left-handedness was nothing more than silly superstition and unwarranted prejudice. There's nothing in the Bible against people using their left hands. We can write and ask him, if you like. Meanwhile you will allow Jamie to use whichever hand he prefers or I shall take action for the wounds he's received."

I hated when she spoke with such big words; I couldn't follow it. Jamie's teacher said, suspiciously, "When were you at Oxford?"

"I graduated 1931," Miss Smith replied.

The teacher looked flustered, but she didn't back down all the way. "You're not to come into my classroom without knocking," she said. "It isn't allowed."

"I won't again so long as I have no cause," Miss Smith said. She hugged Jamie to her, then stood. "I'll be asking Jamie. I don't want him ridiculed, looked down upon, or punished in any way for using his left hand."

The teacher sniffed. Miss Smith stood, and guided me to follow her out. I wanted to wait in the hall to be sure the teacher didn't immediately tie Jamie back up, but Miss Smith said we needed to leave. "I've knocked her pride a bit," she said. "We need to let her get it back."

I didn't see why. I said, "I could have told them he hates being tied." But I didn't really understand why the teacher tied him, and I said so.

Miss Smith sighed. "Ada, which hand do you eat with? When you hold a fork?"

I held up my right hand. "This one."

"Why? Why not use both?"

"This one feels better," I said.

"That's right. And Jamie eats with his other hand, his left hand. He always does. That hand feels better to him."

I guess he did, but I'd never noticed. I'd never cared. "So?"

"So he's learning to write now, and it's much harder to write with the hand you don't eat with. I'll show you, when we get home." She opened the main door of the school, and we went out. A chill wind swirled some dead leaves around the steps. "In the Bible the good people stand on God's right, and the bad people stand on the left, before they get cast into hell. So some—people—"

"Idjits," I supplied.

"Yes." She smiled at me. "Some idiots think left-handedness comes from the devil. It doesn't. It comes from the brain."

"Like that man you were talking about," I said.

"What? Oh, Dr. Goudge. Yes, he's Regius Professor of Divinity at Oxford University. Where I studied."

"And he's left-handed, like Jamie?"

Miss Smith snorted. "I've no idea. I didn't read Divinity. I never met the man."

She'd lied. I looked at her sideways. "So you didn't go to Oxford," I said. Wherever that was, whatever it meant.

"Of course I did," she said. "I studied maths."

We walked down the road. "Is a clubfoot like that?" I asked.

"Like being left-handed? In a way. It's something you're born with."

"No, I mean, is it what that teacher said? A—a mark of the devil." It would explain everything, I thought.

"Ada, of course not! How could you think so?"

I shrugged. "I thought maybe that was why Mam hated me."

Miss Smith's hand touched my shoulder. When she spoke, her voice was uneven. "She doesn't—I'm sure it's not—" She stopped walking and turned to face me. "I don't know what to say," she said, after a pause. "I don't want to tell you a lie, and I don't know the truth."

It was maybe the most honest thing anyone had ever said to me.

"If she does hate you she's wrong to do so," Miss Smith said.

I shook that off. It didn't matter, did it?

Leaves skittered around the tips of my crutches. My bad foot swung in the air. I started down the road again, and after a moment Miss Smith followed.

"Will you ride Butter when we get home?" she asked.

"I think so," I said. "I still can't make him trot."

"Persistence," Miss Smith said. "That's what Lady Thorton says."

I'd asked. Persistence meant to keep trying.

Chapter 19

The very next day, before Jamie went to school, Miss Smith took us to the post office to register for our identity cards. It was a war thing. We would all get cards to carry with us, so that if the Germans invaded, the government could tell who was German and who was English by asking to see our identity cards.

They could also tell because the Germans would be speaking a different language. That's what Miss Smith said. While we stood in line, she explained that all over the world people spoke different, not just different the way I sounded different from Miss Smith and Maggie, but different like actual different words. Jamie wanted to hear different words, so Miss Smith told us some. She said they were in Latin, the only other language she knew. "But it's a dead language," she said. "Nobody speaks it anymore."

Clearly this wasn't true, since she just had been speaking it, but I didn't say so. Jamie asked, "If we kill all the Germans, then their language will be dead. Bam!" He pretended to shoot a German.

Miss Smith pursed her lips, but we'd gotten to the front of the line, so she didn't reprimand him. Instead she told the registry man her name, her birthday, and that she wasn't married and didn't have a job.

Then she pushed us forward. "Ada Smith and James Smith," she said. "They're living with me."

The registry man smiled. "Niece and nevvy, are they? Must be nice to have family staying. I can see the resemblance, sure enough. The girl has your eyes."

"No," Miss Smith said. "They're evacuees. The surname is just a coincidence. I don't know their birth dates," she continued. "It wasn't on their paperwork, and the children couldn't tell me."

The man frowned. "A great big lass and lad like that, and they don't know their own birthdays? Are they simple?"

I stuck my right foot behind my left, and stared at the floor.

"Of course not," Miss Smith snapped. "What an ignorant thing to say."

The man didn't seem put off by her tone. "Well, that's very nice, I'm sure," he said, "but what am I supposed to put down on the form? The government wants proper birth days. There isn't a spot for 'don't know.'"

"Write down April 5, 1929, for Ada," Miss Smith said. After asking me how much I could remember about Jamie being a baby, she'd decided long ago I must be ten. "For Jamie put February 15." She looked down at us. "Nineteen thirty-three," she said. "We're pretty sure he's six years old."

The man raised an eyebrow, but did as she told him.

"What's all that mean?" I asked, when we were back out on the street.

"Birthdays are days you get presents," Jamie said gloomily, "and cake for tea. And at school you get to wear the birthday hat."

I remembered Miss Smith asking us about birthdays, when we first came to her, but I'd never heard about a birthday hat. Turns out it was a school thing. At Jamie's school his teacher posted birthdays on a big calendar, and when it was your birthday you wore a hat and everybody made a fuss over you.

When Jamie'd said he didn't know his birthday, his class had laughed at him. He hadn't told us that.

"But now we have birthdays," Jamie said contentedly. "What you told the man. I'll tell teacher this afternoon and she'll write it on her calendar." He smiled at Miss Smith. "What was it?"

"February 15, 1933," Miss Smith said.

"It's not your real birthday," I said.

"Close enough," Miss Smith said. "February 15 was my father's birthday. Jamie can use it."

"Is your father dead?"

"No," Miss Smith said. "At least, not so I've heard. I think my brothers would tell me. It doesn't matter if Jamie shares. There are only 365 days in the year, and there are a lot more people in the world than that. Lots of people have the same birthdays."

"But it isn't Jamie's real birthday," I said.

"No, it's not." Miss Smith turned and bent over so she was looking directly at me. "When I find out your real birthdays, I'll change your identity cards. Okay? Promise."

"Okay." I didn't mind a temporary lie. "How do you find out?"

Miss Smith's nostrils narrowed. "Your mother knows. When she answers my letters, she'll tell us."

Could be a long time, then. I doubted I'd ever go to school and wear a birthday hat, but still— "Will we have cake for tea on my birthday? On the day you told the man?"

"Yes," Miss Smith said. A sudden look of sadness washed over her face, then disappeared so quickly that if I hadn't been looking right at her, I never would have seen it. *Sadness?* I thought. *How did I know that was sadness? And why would Miss Smith be sad?*

"That was Becky's birthday," Miss Smith said. "It'll be nice to have a reason to celebrate the day again."

"That's a lie," I said. I wasn't angry about it, but it was one.

"Oh." Miss Smith forced a laugh. "It is and it isn't. It will be hard for me, but I'd like very much to be happy again."

Chapter 20

Stephen White and his colonel invited me to tea. They sent me a proper invitation, written out, by post, and Miss Smith handed it to me without opening it. I stared and stared at the marks on the paper, but I couldn't make sense of them. Neither could Jamie, no matter how hard he tried. "The writing's wiggly," he said. "Not like in books."

So I had to ask Miss Smith, which made me angry. She read it out—tea, Stephen and the colonel, Saturday, October 7—and all the while I grew angrier and angrier that I couldn't read the words myself. Miss Smith looked up at me and laughed. "Ada, what a face!" she said. "It's your own fault. I'm happy to teach you."

Easy for her to laugh. What if I tried and found out I really couldn't learn?

"I'll write back an answer for you," Miss Smith said. "You want to go, don't you?"

"No," I said. I didn't want her having to write for me.

"Why not? You'll have something nice to eat, I'm sure, and Stephen's your friend. The colonel's an old man, but he's kind and has some interesting stories."

"No!" I said. I added, "Stephen's not my friend."

Miss Smith sat down and looked at me. "You told me he carried you to the train station," she said. "That sounds like something a friend would do."

Maybe.

"The way you helped Margaret Thorton when she was hurt. You were a friend to her the way Stephen was a friend to you."

I did want to count Maggie as a friend. I guessed I wouldn't mind counting Stephen as one, only it was harder to be friends with someone who helped you than someone you'd helped.

"I know you know how to behave nicely," Miss Smith continued. "You did when we went out for tea the other day. And I'd walk you to the colonel's house, and pick you up again when you were through. You wouldn't be there very long. Perhaps an hour. You'd have a treat and a cup of tea, and talk. That would be all."

I scowled. "Why do you want me to go?"

She sighed, air coming out her nose so she sounded like Butter. "I don't. I don't care what you do. Only

I thought you'd like to be around someone your own age, for a change, and I was happy for you that you'd gotten the invitation."

I swallowed. I didn't feel happy. I felt something else. Scared? I didn't know. "I don't want to go," I said. "You don't have to write anything."

"I have to write and decline the invitation," Miss Smith said. "You've got to answer, either way."

I hadn't known that, of course. I kicked at the chair leg with my good foot while she got out paper and a pen. She wrote something down, then shoved it toward me. "That says: 'Miss Smith regrets that she is unable to accept your kind invitation for October seventh.' That's how you say no politely. And quit kicking the chair."

I kicked harder. I didn't care if I was polite or not. "I don't need the colonel staring at my foot," I said.

"How could he?" Miss Smith asked. She grabbed my good foot and held it still. "I said, stop it. And the colonel wouldn't be staring at you under any circumstances. He can't see much of anything. He's gone blind."

On the actual day of the seventh it rained, cold and hard. I couldn't ride. Miss Smith gave Jamie scissors and a magazine with pictures of planes in it, and he was happy cutting them out and then flying them around the rug. I didn't have anything to do. "I couldn't have gone to that stupid tea anyhow," I said.

Miss Smith looked up from her sewing machine. She'd found some old towels and was turning them into dressing gowns for Jamie and me. Dressing gowns were like coats you put on over your pajamas in winter when you weren't in bed. It wasn't winter cold yet, but it was cold enough that Miss Smith had lit the coal fire in the living room. That and the kitchen range kept the house warm.

"We'd have used my big umbrella," Miss Smith said. "You still could have gone."

"Can I go now?" I asked.

Miss Smith shook her head. "Once you've given your answer you can't change your mind," she said. "It's not polite."

"I don't care about polite!"

"Maybe not," she said, crisply, "but the colonel does, and tea parties are about being polite."

I stomped my crutch. It landed on one of Jamie's paper planes, smashing it into the rug. Jamie howled. I didn't care.

Miss Smith got up. "What's wrong with you?"

"My stomach hurts!"

"You're angry," she said. "But you can't take it out

on Jamie. Say you're sorry and see if you can fix that plane."

"I'm not sorry," I said.

Miss Smith pressed her eyes shut. "Say it anyhow," she said.

"No!"

"Jamie, come here." Miss Smith sat down on the sofa and opened her arms, and Jamie crawled into her lap. Ever since she'd hugged him in his classroom, he'd been cuddling up to her. I could hardly stand it. "Your sister's having a hard time," Miss Smith told him. "She didn't mean to rip your plane."

I wanted to say, I did too, only it was such a lie. I never meant to hurt Jamie. He just sometimes got in the way. But looking at him curled up on Miss Smith's lap made me want to scream. Nobody did that for me.

Except that Miss Smith patted the space beside her. "Sit down," she said. "No, really. Sit."

And then she put her arm around me, and pulled me halfway over.

She did.

I was almost on her lap.

"You're so stiff," she said. "It's like trying to comfort a piece of wood."

It felt very odd to have her touch me. Of course it made me tense. But I didn't go away inside my head.

I sat on the sofa with Miss Smith's arm around me, and Jamie breathing soft near my shoulder, and I watched the coal fire flicker, and I stayed right there, right there in that room, and none of us moved for half an hour. Jamie fell asleep, and Miss Smith and I just sat, neither of us saying a word, until it was time to put the blackout up, and make tea.

Chapter 21

Butter refused to ever do anything but walk.

I was nice to him. I tried hard not to smack him, even when his laziness angered me. I brought him treats, and I brushed him every day, and sometimes when I rode him I dropped the reins on his neck and just let him wander around the pasture however he liked. When I stood at the corner gate and called his name, he came right to me, every time, and he stood without being tied while I brushed him and put his bridle on. I knew he liked me. He really did. But he wouldn't go faster, no matter what. He wouldn't run, and until he would run, I knew we'd never be able to jump.

I was afraid Lady Thorton hadn't meant it when she said I could ask Mr. Grimes for help, but in the end I decided I had to take the chance.

"I'm going to visit Mr. Grimes," I said at lunch one day. It was a cold day; I was glad to be wearing one of Maggie's old sweaters.

Miss Smith gave me an eye. "How and why?"

"I'll ride Butter," I said.

Miss Smith stared.

"I do ride him quite a bit," I said. "We get on well He's a very nice pony. He wouldn't mind taking me there."

"Ada," Miss Smith said, "I may be negligent, but I am not blind. I'm well aware how much you ride that pony."

"Yes, miss," I said.

"I've told you and told you to call me Susan," she said. "Your refusal to do so is starting to feel like an affront. Why do you want to visit Mr. Grimes?"

"I just want to," I said. "He was nice to me. *Susan,*" I added.

She rolled her eyes. "And?" she prompted.

"And I'm having trouble with Butter and I don't know what I'm doing wrong. I can't hardly get him to move. Miss—the iron-face—I mean, Maggie's mum—"

"Lady Thorton," prompted Miss Smith.

"Yeah. Her. She said if I had trouble I could ask Mr. Grimes for help."

Miss Smith picked up a piece of carrot with her fork. She put it into her mouth and chewed slowly. "It hardly sounds like Butter," she said. "When I rode him he was quite keen, and he's not gotten that much older." She picked up another piece of carrot. "All right," she said, after she'd chewed it and swallowed. "You may go. Do you remember how to get there?"

I nodded. It was easy, just the two turns, plus there was a fancy fence and iron gates at the start of the drive. Couldn't miss those.

Miss Smith said, "If you're going to be riding out on the road, it might be better if you put a saddle on him. You could take the right stirrup off, so it wouldn't bang against his side." She knew I wouldn't be able to use the right stirrup. It would hurt too much.

"Is his the little one?" I asked. There were three saddles in the storage room, hung on racks and covered with cloth. Two were the same size and one was smaller.

"Yes," Miss Smith said. "I'll show you."

"'S all right," I said. "I don't need you."

She looked at me for a long time. "I never know what to do for the two of you," she said at last. "I should have gone to Jamie's school earlier. I probably should supervise you more. But you'd hate it, wouldn't you?"

I didn't think this was the sort of question that needed an answer. I got up and scraped my plate into the trash, then filled the sink with soapy water to do the dishes.

"Will you at least tell me if you're having trouble? Ask, if you need help?"

I didn't look at her. "I won't need help," I said.

Behind me Miss Smith sighed. "Have it your way," she said at last.

The saddle was awkward but I got it on him. I started to climb on, and the whole saddle shifted to one side. I got off, put it right, and tightened the girth again—it had gone loose, I didn't know why. The second time I climbed aboard it stayed steady. We went through the gate and ambled down the road.

The airfield no longer showed any traces of the explosion or the burned plane. Jamie'd said three people died, but he didn't know them. In the last week more huts had gone up at the airfield, and one big tower that no one knew what was for. Planes sat parked in rows at the far side of the runway, and one plane kept coming toward the runway, touching down for a moment, and then rising into the air again. Round and round in loops. Butter barely flicked an ear at it. To him, planes landing and taking off had become common as trees.

Partway down the road Butter balked, and wanted to turn and go back home. I made him continue. He went stubborn after that, mouthing the bit and flicking his ears at me, as though cursing me in some low horse language. He walked slower than ever, and I thought with longing of Jonathan's horse. A month ago I'd been thrilled with Butter, and now I wanted something more.

Two months ago I'd not seen trees.

Eventually we made it to Maggie's house, and around to the stable yard. Mr. Grimes was there in the yard, rinsing a big gray horse with water from a bucket. "Aye," he said when he saw me.

"Aye," I said back, suddenly feeling shy. He hadn't said I could visit—only Maggie's mum had said that, and maybe Mr. Grimes wouldn't like it. I slid off Butter and put my right foot behind my left.

Mr. Grimes looked me up and down. "Wait there," he said. He put the horse he was tending into a stall. "Now," he said, coming toward me, "explain what you were doing riding this poor animal down the road."

"I wanted help," I said. "I can't make him go."

"I should think not." He bent toward Butter's forefeet. "Hasn't had his feet trimmed in years, has he? Bet not since that other one died. That Miss Becky." He stalked off, and came back with his hands full of metal tools. "You just hold him," he said. He cradled Butter's hoof upside down in his hand, and then with a sort of pincher thing he *cut Butter's hoof right off.*

I screamed. Butter startled. Mr. Grimes straightened, dropping Butter's foot. Butter still had quite a bit of hoof left, I saw. But the cut-off part lay on the cobbled yard, curved and thick and horrible-looking. Mr. Grimes said, "Does it look like I'm hurting him?"

It didn't. I couldn't believe it. Butter stood perfectly calm.

"Ponies' hooves are like our fingernails," he said. He picked up another tool and rasped Butter's short hoof smooth. "They grow and they have to be trimmed."

Miss Smith was a bear for having our fingernails trimmed. She'd trimmed them the second day we were with her, and our toenails too, and she kept on us to trim them every week. With clippers, not just nibbling off the broken bits like I was used to. It was strange, but Mr. Grimes was right, it didn't hurt.

"His are so overgrown they're hurting him," Mr. Grimes continued, moving on to Butter's other front foot. "Probably hurts him to walk at all, and he couldn't really go faster, not without tripping himself. He's showing sense. This ought to make a big difference."

I felt stung. I'd been hurting him, and I didn't know.

"Some people shouldn't own ponies," Mr. Grimes said, as though echoing my thoughts. Then he looked at me. "I don't mean you," he said. "Comin' from London, and bein' your age and all, how could you know? But that Miss Smith, she just threw the pony into the field once she'd sold Miss Becky's hunters, and she's never looked at him again as far as I can tell."

"She told me ponies could do fine just eating grass."

"Aye, that's true, but it's not the only thing they need. If someone gave you enough to eat, but didn't keep you clean or healthy or ever show you any kind of love, how would you feel?"

I said, "I wouldn't feel hungry."

Mr. Grimes laughed. "Well, that's so." When he was finished he said, "You bring him back here in four weeks or so, so I can trim him again. Usually you'd say every six weeks, but we'll have a bit of work to do before he's back to normal. Ordinarily the village farrier'd do it, but he enlisted last week."

I nodded. Searched my head for the right words to say. Found them. "Thank you very much, Mr. Grimes."

His eyes crinkled, but he didn't smile. He pulled off his hat, revealing a nearly bald head, and scratched himself behind one ear. "It's just Grimes," he said. "Mr. Grimes, that would be if I were a butler or something important, like. But if we're going to be friends, you can call me Fred."

"Fred." I held out my hand, the way the colonel had. Fred shook it.

"And you're?" he prompted.

"Ada," I said. "Ada Smith, but just Ada to you."

Fred took me all around the pony. He cut Butter's long tangled mane ("normally we'd pull it, not cut it, but this mess is hopeless") and showed me how to start untangling his tail. He taught me how to clean the saddle and bridle, and how to oil them, over and over with tiny dollops of oil on a rag. "You keep doing that," he said. "And any other tack you see at Miss Smith's, you oil that too. Leather dries out. It'll be ruined if it goes neglected much longer."

Then he told me he had to get on working. "Too much to do these days," he said. "We've had to put the hunters back to grass. Too much for one man to keep 'em legged up and properly strapped and all, and anyways, there's no hunting with the war on. But even still, it's nearly all I can do, caring for thirteen horses."

"I can help," I said.

"Aye, I'd be grateful," he said. We'd already put Butter into an empty stall while I worked on the tack. I helped grain, hay, and water the horses, bad foot and all, and he didn't say a word about my limping or expect me not to be able to do things. When we were finished I saddled and bridled Butter. Fred gave me a leg into the saddle.

"Maggie said horses could have clubfoot," I said. "She said you could fix it." I tried not to feel hopeful.

"Aye," he said. "In horses you fix it with special shoes. It's not like clubfoot in people, though. I don't think. That's what you've got?"

I nodded. "Can't help you," he said. "But I'll help you otherwise, whenever you like. You come back."

I went down the drive. I turned left at the road, which I knew was correct, but after that I'm not sure what happened. It should have been easy to find Miss Smith's house. Instead I got lost.

Chapter 22

Seeing the ocean was like seeing grass for the first time.

I'd been lost for a while, wandering unfamiliar lanes. When I first realized I didn't know where I was, I tried to retrace my steps back to Maggie's, but I ended up somewhere else entirely. I tried letting Butter show me the way, but every time I gave him his head, he put it down and started to graze. He was no use. I kept moving, searching for something familiar. Finally I saw a long, tall hill and climbed it, thinking perhaps I could recognize Miss Smith's house, or at least the village, from above.

Instead I saw, stretched out in the distance, an endless carpet of blue and gray. Clouds floated over it, and small white things seemed to flicker on the surface of it, but mostly it was like grass, flat and broad and unchanging, except that it went on forever, farther out than I could see. It made me feel lost and shivery, looking at it. I stared and stared. What could it be?

Eventually I pulled my gaze down from it, and there was the village—I recognized the church spire. So close to that gray-blue expanse. How had I not known? I made my way down the hill, scrabbling through rough tall grass, but keeping Butter's head in the direction of the steeple. Then we found a road, and kept going. Pretty soon I was riding right along the middle of the main street. The village was quiet, the shops all shut up. The sky was getting dark, and of course not a light showed anywhere. Above me came the roar of an airplane.

At home Miss Smith and Jamie rushed out the door when they saw Butter and me walking up the lane.

"I didn't mean to," I said. "I got lost."

Miss Smith said, "I thought you'd fallen off that pony and were lying dead in a ditch somewhere."

Jamie's face went white.

"I wouldn't have died," I said. I went around to the back to take care of Butter. Jamie helped me.

"How was school?" I asked.

He shrugged.

"Teacher let you use your left hand?"

"Only because Susan made her. She still thinks

I've got the mark of the devil." He held my hand as we walked back to the house. "When you weren't here Susan didn't say you were dead in a ditch. She said you were probably having a nice time and I shouldn't worry." He paused. "She was worried, though. I could tell."

I snorted. "She doesn't need to worry. Nor you."

Dinner was waiting. I fell to eating, so hungry that for a few minutes I didn't think of anything else. Then I said, "I saw something strange from the top of the hill. Far away. Like grass, stretched out a long way, and flat, but different—blue and gray. When the sun hit it, it looked shiny."

"That's the ocean," Miss Smith said. "The English Channel. I told you before we weren't far from it."

I stared at her. I wanted to say she hadn't told me anything. I wanted to say she'd crippled my pony, ignoring him. I wanted to say she should have showed us the ocean, she should have taken us there.

I wanted to say she never needed to worry about either of us. She didn't need to bother. I could take care of Jamie, and I could take care of myself. I always had.

I wanted to say a lot of things, but, as usual, I didn't have the words for the thoughts inside my head. I dropped my head and went back to eating.

"Did Grimes help you?" Miss Smith asked.

"Yes," I said, rudely, through a mouthful of food.

"Why wouldn't Butter trot?"

I swallowed. I took a deep breath. I said, "Because you crippled him."

Miss Smith looked up, sharp. "Explain."

I didn't want to talk, but eventually she got the whole story out of me. She sighed. "Well, I am sorry. It was ignorance, not deliberate abuse—but that's never an excuse, is it?" She reached out to pat my arm, but I jerked away. "I understand why you're angry with me," she said. "I'd be angry too."

After dinner she marched me out to the pasture. She made me show her what Butter's feet looked like now, and tell her how they had been. She made me tell her what else Grimes had taught me, and then she went into the storage room and looked at all the tack. "It's awful having to face your own shortcomings," she said. "Did Butter feel better after he had his feet fixed?"

"They're not fixed," I said. "They won't be fixed for weeks and weeks. And I don't know how he felt. I got *lost*."

She nodded. "You must have been scared. Scared and angry."

"Of course not," I said, though I had been, at least until I'd seen the sea. "Of course I wasn't scared."

"Angry," Susan said, putting her arm around me.

"No," I said through clenched teeth. But I was. Oh, I was.

Chapter 23

The *Royal Oak* sank.

She was a Royal Navy battleship. She was torpe-
doed by a German submarine while anchored off the
coast of Scotland, and 833 of the over twelve hundred men on her died. We heard about it on the radio,
which we listened to most nights.

The next Saturday Susan decided to take us to
the movies. It was the first time Jamie and I had ever
been. We sat down on the plush seats, like our purple
chairs at home, and before we knew it the whole wall in
front of us had become a giant moving picture. Music
played, and a man's voice started to talk about the war.

I'd thought we were going to watch a story, not
stuff about the war. Other than the silly posters and
the sandbags that lay piled near some of the road
intersections, you'd hardly know there was a war.
Hadn't been any bombs. But now here was a picture
of an enormous ship, rolling onto its side while black

smoke poured out of holes in its hull. The picture was so big and so horrible, and it got worse when the solemn voice talking about the *Royal Oak* said that over a hundred of the dead were young boys. I looked at Jamie sitting on Susan's other side. "I want to go home," I whispered.

"Shh," Susan said. "The newsreel will be over in a minute. Then they'll show the story."

"I want to go home," I said, more loudly.

"Don't start," Susan said.

"Don't start," Jamie echoed.

I didn't. But I plugged my ears and I shut my eyes, and I stayed that way until Susan nudged me to let me know the story picture was starting. Even then I couldn't quit thinking about the burning ship and the boys that died.

I had nightmares from the pictures. Jamie wet the bed, but he always did, every night still. I had dreams of fire and smoke and being tied to my chair, my little chair in our flat at home. I couldn't walk and I couldn't move, and I screamed. Jamie woke and cried and Susan came at a run.

"So, that was a little too overwhelming?" Susan said the next morning. She looked tired and cross, but she usually looked cross in the mornings.

I avoided her gaze. I didn't know what she meant by *overwhelming*.

"A little too much?" Susan said.

Of course it was too much. It was 833 men too much.

Susan sighed. "Next time we go to the movies we'll wait in the lobby until the newsreel's over. I assume that the radio's still okay?"

I nodded. The radio didn't come with pictures.

Jamie told Susan his teacher still thought he had the devil in him, and because of that we had to start going to church on Sundays.

"Of course you haven't got the devil in you," she said, "but if you go it'll give the gossips one less thing to talk about. Besides, I've been feeling guilty about neglecting your religious education."

She made us go, but *she didn't*. She went the first time only, to show us how you had to sit in the pew, and stay quiet, unless there was singing or words to say, in which case we still sat quiet because we didn't know the songs or the words. A man up front read stories and then talked a long time, and Jamie got in trouble for kicking the pew. That was what the benches were called. Pews. Jamie thought it was a funny word. The whole next week he held his nose and said "Pew!" every time he sat down.

After the first Sunday Susan walked us to the church, then took a walk through the village and picked us up on her way back. She said churches and her didn't agree.

"You said your father worked in the church," I said, scowling, on our way home the second Sunday. The lady beside Jamie and me had spent the whole sitting-down part of the service staring at us, and I hadn't liked it at all.

Miss Smith looked tight-lipped. "Yes. My father has made it clear he doesn't think I can be redeemed."

Jamie said, "What's that mean? *Redeemed?*"

"In my case being redeemed means changing my evil ways and regaining my heavenly crown. It means my parents don't like me. And yes, my father's still alive. My mother died."

"Oh." Jamie threw a rock, and hit a fencepost half a block away. "Our mam doesn't like us either. 'Specially Ada. She hates Ada. Ada's not redeemed."

I flinched. "Maybe I am now. Maybe now I can walk."

"Not without crutches," Jamie said. "You've still got that ugly foot."

"Jamie!" Susan said. "You apologize!"

Jamie said, "But she does!"

"Her foot isn't ugly," Miss Smith said. "What a horrid thing to say! And Ada, you've done nothing wrong. Your foot is not your fault. You don't need to be redeemed."

I watched the tips of my crutches as we went down the road. Crutches, good foot, crutches, good foot. Ugly foot skimming along in the air. Always there, no matter what anyone said.

Chapter 24

Butter galloped. He trotted first, and that was so bouncy I had to hold on to his mane so I didn't fall off. But I kept kicking him, and he trotted faster and faster, until suddenly everything evened out, and he was cantering. If I kept kicking him from there, he went faster still, until my eyes watered and the wind made noise in my ears. That was galloping. It was the best.

I tried to jump the stone wall of Butter's pasture. I galloped him the length of the field, hard as I could, and steered him right toward the wall. He got close, closer, then slammed his feet into the ground. He stopped dead. I kept going, straight over his ears. I missed hitting the base of the wall, but not by much.

Susan came running into the field. I hadn't known she was watching me. "Stop that, you idiot," she said.

I looked at her. Butter was snorting and tossing his

head, and I figured I'd better have another go at the wall quickly, before I lost my nerve.

"You don't have the first clue what you're doing," Susan continued. "You get on over to Fred Grimes and get him to teach you something before you get yourself killed. Putting that poor pony at a three-foot wall, when he's hardly ever jumped in his life!"

"He hasn't?" I asked. I figured all horses knew how to jump walls. Jonathan's horse hadn't had any trouble with it.

"He hasn't," she said. She rubbed the end of Butter's nose. "You'll hurt him if you aren't careful. You'll scare him, and that'll put him off jumping forever. Not to mention what it might do to you."

She should talk about hurting the pony. Ignoring him until he was practically crippled. He'd been better as soon as his hooves were trimmed. Better the very next day.

"Yes, I know what you're thinking," she continued. "But I know what he needs now and I won't hurt him again. You know what you need now too, because I'm telling you. You get on over to Fred Grimes."

So I went on over to see Fred in the stables behind Maggie's house. He agreed to watch me ride, and help me, for a bit of time after his lunch two days a week. In exchange I'd work for him the rest of the afternoon. Susan gave me a map she'd drawn, and showed me how to trace my route on it, so I wouldn't be lost again. I tied my crutches to the back of the saddle so I had them for doing chores.

Fred taught me to kick less. He taught me to use one leg only to ask for a canter, so that I didn't have to get bounced by the trot. He tried to teach me to post to the trot—to rise and fall to the motion smoothly, without bouncing—but that was hard with only one stirrup. He taught me more about steering, and when he was happy with my progress he set up little poles in the field beyond the stable yard and had me practice going over them. It was a long way from jumping the stone wall. Fred said I wasn't to try that on Butter until he told me I was ready.

Stephen White's colonel sent another invitation to tea. I declined. "Idiot girl," Susan grumbled.

Meanwhile the war had become an endless stream of pamphlets the government sent through the mail. How to wear your gas mask. Why to carry your gas mask. How not to get hit by a car in the blackout. (You could carry a flashlight, if you covered over the glass with tissue paper; you should paint curbs white so the people driving the cars could see them.) Why you should give the government your excess pots and pans. (They wanted to make planes from them. Susan refused to do it. She said she had exactly as many pans as she needed. This made Jamie so upset that eventually she relented, and gave him an old nasty chip pan to turn in.)

There weren't any bombs. What there were was German submarines, circling all of England, trying to blow up any ships heading in or out of her harbors.

This was a big problem, Susan said, because England didn't grow enough food. Most of the food English people ate was shipped in from other countries. Already there was less food in the shops, and what was there cost more, though Susan said some of that was because the summer was over. We wouldn't see as many fresh fruits and vegetables until next spring.

You never saw anyone more interested in fruits and vegetables than Susan. We were all the time having to eat strange things. Brussels sprouts. Turnips. Leeks. Peaches, which I loved, but also prunes, which I didn't. Prunes came in cans and were slimy going down.

Every week that went by without bombs, more evacuees returned to London. Even the ones living with Lady Thorton had gone. In the village Lady Thorton fussed about it, but she couldn't stop parents from sending for their children. "London will be bombed," she insisted.

Mam never wrote, so Susan was still stuck with us. When I said so she gave me an odd look. "Your mother's smart to keep you here, where it's safer," she said. "But I wish she'd answer my letters. I find her silence hard to understand."

By the start of November so many children had returned to London that Jamie's teacher left too. His class was combined with the other primary class. His new teacher didn't think he had the devil in him. She said so. She didn't care at all if he wrote with his left hand.

He still wet the bed.

I thought it was mostly habit by now. Susan had a rubber sheet to protect the mattress, but she was tired of cleaning the regular sheets. I was tired of waking up to the dampness and the smell. Neither of us said so to Jamie. He was ashamed, I knew.

Lady Thorton wanted Susan to join the Women's Volunteer Service, the WVS. She came to tea and told Susan she needed her help.

"No one needs my help," Susan said. "Besides, I'm busy taking care of these children."

Lady Thorton cut her eyes at me. Jamie was at

school, but I'd come in from the pasture to have tea. It wasn't one of my days for helping Fred. "This one doesn't seem to need much care," Lady Thorton said.

"You'd be surprised," Susan said.

I felt cross. I didn't need her. Plus, she still spent part of each day lying around, staring at nothing. I said, "It's not like you have a proper job."

Susan glared at me. Lady Thorton laughed out loud. Then Lady Thorton said, gesturing to the sewing machine still set up in the corner of the room, "We could use you to sew bed jackets for soldiers. All sorts of sewing, actually."

Susan shook her head. "You all don't like me," she said. "The women in this village never liked me."

Lady Thorton pressed her lips together. She set her teacup down. "That's not true," she said.

Susan looked cross. "Don't be patronizing," she said. "Becky got along with your set because of the horses, but that's all."

"You never gave anyone a chance," Lady Thorton said. "Most of the village came to the funeral."

"Oh, the funeral! Bunch of nosy busybodies!"

"I think you should make an effort," Lady Thorton said. "You might be surprised. And—it's good to be seen helping the war effort, don't you agree? This isn't the time to be isolationist."

I had been listening closely. I asked, "What's that mean?"

Lady Thorton said, "An isolationist is someone who doesn't support the war. Someone who wants us to stand apart; someone who doesn't care about things."

I said, "But she *doesn't* care about things."

Susan looked like I'd slapped her. "How can you say that? Of course I do!"

I shrugged.

"Is feeding you three meals a day not caring for you?" she demanded. "No, don't you look away. You look at me, Ada. When I confronted Jamie's teacher— wasn't that caring for him?"

Who knew she'd get so wound up? I tried to look away, but she put her hand under my chin and turned my face back toward her. "Wasn't it?" she insisted.

I didn't want to answer, but I knew she wouldn't let go of me until I did. "Maybe," I said at last.

She released me and turned back to Lady Thorton, who was looking amused. "I'll join," she said.

As soon as Lady Thorton left, Susan told me off. "What did you mean by complaining that I haven't got a proper job? What sort of job do you expect me to have?"

I shrugged. It surprised me, how she could go on buying food without working, even though she did get paid for taking us. "Mam works in the pub," I said.

"Well, I'm not doing that," she said. "I did try to get a job, when I first moved here with Becky. No one would have me. Oxford degree or not. Any position I was qualified for was reserved for men. Can't have a woman stealing a man's job, now, can we?"

I didn't understand why we were having this conversation.

"Oh!" she continued. "Me, in the WVS! All those wretched do-gooders! What nonsense."

"Why do soldiers need bed jackets?" I asked. I wasn't sure what a bed jacket was.

"Who knows," Susan said. "They're for hurt soldiers, I'd say. Ones that have to go to hospital."

I hadn't heard of any hurt soldiers. "The ones that get blown up in the ocean fall into the water and die," I said.

"I suppose so," Susan said, shuddering. "But there are different kinds of battles. Some hurt soldiers survive."

A few days later Susan got her WVS uniform. She put it on to go to her first meeting. She looked nice in it. She wore stockings, and leather shoes with heels.

"Quit staring," she said as she pulled on her gloves. "You could come with me. A junior member. Or perhaps a token evacuee."

I shook my head. While she was gone I thought I might try out the sewing machine. Or cook something. The weather was wretched; I didn't want to ride. "Why are you scared?" I asked her.

She made a face. "All those proper housewives! I don't fit in. I never have."

"You've got the uniform," I said.

She made another face. "True. But it's not the outside that counts, not with that group. Oh, well." She went away to her meeting.

I stayed home and broke her sewing machine.

Chapter 25

I didn't mean to. I'd watched Susan using it, and it
looked easy, and all I was trying to do was sew two
scraps of fabric together, for a start. But the scraps
sucked into the bottom part of the machine, and the
needle ran up and down through it anyway. A bunch
of thread came out of nowhere, snarling itself into a
knot, and then the machine made an awful noise and
then the needle snapped in two.

I took my foot off the pedal. I stared at the tangle
of thread and cloth, at the broken stump of the needle. I was going to get in awful trouble. Susan had
been sewing every day since she finished our dressing gowns. She'd made herself a dress and made new
shorts for Jamie. She loved the sewing machine.

I couldn't think what to do. My stomach roiled. I
fled upstairs and hid in the spare room, the room still
full of Becky's things. I slid under the bed, deep into
the corner. My mind went numb. I started to shake.

Much later I heard Susan come in the front door. Heard her calling my name, heard Jamie climbing the stairs. He opened the door to our bedroom and shouted, "She's not up here!"

"She has to be." That was Susan's voice. "Her crutches are right by the stairs."

They called my name, over and over. Jamie ran outside. Ran back in. It grew darker. Finally Susan's face poked under the edge of the bed. "You idiot girl! Why are you hiding?"

I cringed against the far wall. Susan grabbed my arm and dragged me out. "What's wrong? Who frightened you?"

I threw my hands over my head. "I'm not going to hit you!" Susan shouted. "Stop that!"

Jamie came into the room. "Was it the Germans?" he asked.

"Of course it wasn't the Germans," Susan said. "Ada. Ada!" She had an iron grip on my wrists, pulling my arms down. *What happened?*

"You'll send me back," I said. "You'll send me back." All that time under the bed my panic had grown worse and worse. I'd lose Butter. Freedom. *Jamie.*

"I won't send you back," Susan said. "But you'll tell me this instant what's wrong." She put a finger under my chin. "Look at me. Now, tell me."

I looked at her, but only for a second. I squirmed away from her grasp. Finally I gasped, "I broke your sewing machine."

Susan sighed. "Look at me," she said. She tipped my chin up again. "You tried to use my sewing machine?"

I nodded. Squirmed away. Looked at the ground.

She tipped my chin up. "And you broke it?"

I nodded. Looking her in the eye was nearly impossible. "It's okay," she said. "No matter what, it's okay."

I couldn't believe her. It wasn't going to be okay.

"You did do something wrong," she said. "You should have asked me first. But you don't need to be so afraid. I'm not going to hurt you because you made a mistake. Let's go see how badly it's broken."

She made me go down the stairs to the living room. The fire was lit and the room was growing warm. It turned out that I'd only broken the needle, not the entire machine. Needles wore out sometimes, Susan said, and you had to replace them anyhow. She had an extra needle, so she took the broken one out and replaced it. Then she removed the snarled mess of cloth and thread. "It really is all right," she said. "Do you want to see what you did wrong?"

I shook my head. My stomach hurt so bad. Susan pulled me over anyhow, and showed me how the machine worked, and how I'd needed to lever the needle into place before I started the machine running. "Tomorrow you can practice," Susan said.

"No thank you," I said.

She pulled me close to her, in a sort of one-armed embrace. "Why did you hide? Why were you under the bed?"

Jamie had been hovering the entire time. "Mam puts her in the cabinet," he said, "whenever she's really bad."

"But why put *yourself* there, Ada? You didn't have to."

So I can stay. SoIcanstaysoIcanstaysoIcanstay.

"I'm not going to shut you up anywhere, no matter what, okay?"

"Okay." My stomach felt awful. My voice sounded very small. I could barely make my mind stay in the room with Susan and Jamie. I said, "I know I have to leave. Please, can Jamie come too?"

"Ada!"

Oh no. Ohnoohnoohnoohno. Without Jamie I would die.

"I'm not going to send you away. Why would I send you away? You made a mistake. A little, small mistake." Now both Susan's arms were around me. I tried to squirm free. She held me tighter. "Did you really think I'd send you away?"

I nodded.

"Let me tell you something. When I was coming back from my meeting, I was thinking, 'Maybe Ada will have made some tea.' I was imagining how you'd have the lights on inside, and the blackout up, and I was thinking how lovely it was to have someone to come home to again. I used to dread going back to an empty house."

"I'm sorry I didn't make tea," I said.

"That's not what I'm trying to tell you," she said. "I'm trying to say that I'm glad you're here."

I couldn't come down from my panic. It took me most of the night before I could really breathe. Susan made tea, and when I couldn't swallow any, she didn't insist. "I half wonder if I ought to give you a slug of brandy," she said. "You'll never sleep in the state you're in." She made me take a hot bath and she tucked the blankets tight around me. She was right: I lay awake half the night. But eventually I slept, and when I woke up, Jamie and I were still there. I could see Butter out the back window. Susan was frying sausages for breakfast and I could breathe again.

Not long after that Jamie came home from school carrying the ugliest cat Susan and I had ever seen. Its filthy, matted hair might have been any color at all beneath the dirt. One eye was swollen shut. It glared at Susan and me out of its other.

"I'm keeping him," Jamie announced, dumping the cat into the middle of the kitchen. It swished its tail and hissed at us. "His name's Bovril. He's hungry."

Bovril was a hot drink Susan made for us most nights. It was nasty, but I'd gotten used to it. It had nothing whatsoever to do with cats.

"You're not keeping it," Susan said. "Pick it up at once and put it out. It's crawling with fleas."

"I am keeping it," Jamie said. He picked the cat up—the cat went limp in his arms. "It's my onager. My own onager. His name's Bovril." He began to go up the stairs.

An onager was an animal from the *Swiss Family Robinson* book. Susan said onagers were like donkeys. You could ride them. They were nothing like cats.

"Don't you dare take that animal into your bedroom," Susan yelled after him.

"I'm not," Jamie said, "I'm giving him a bath."

"Good Lord," Susan said, to me. "We'll have to call an ambulance. It'll scratch him to death."

It didn't. Jamie bathed the mangy cat and drowned its fleas. He brought it back downstairs wrapped in one of Susan's best towels. He fed it part of his meat from dinner.

"It'll hunt for itself after this," Susan said. "I'm not cooking for a cat."

"He's a good hunter," Jamie said, rubbing the cat's head. "Aren't you, Bovril?"

Every night after that, Jamie fell asleep with Bovril curled in his arms. He never wet the bed again. By the end of the second week Susan was offering Bovril saucers of watered milk. "It's worth it," she told me. "Saves me washing all those sheets."

Chapter 26

Susan tricked me into writing.

Jamie was practicing his letters at the table in the evening after the dishes were washed. I sat down at my place and watched him. "Show Ada why you're left-handed," Susan suggested.

Jamie grinned. He moved his pencil from his left hand to his right. Immediately the pencil started to skitter across the page. His letters went from small and neat to large and shaky.

"You're fooling," I said, laughing at his grin.

"I'm not," he said. "I can't do it in this hand."

"You try," Susan suggested. "Try your left hand first." She took a fresh piece of paper and wrote a few letters on it. "Copy that."

I tried, but it *was* impossible. Even when I used my right hand to hold the page steady, my left hand couldn't control the pencil at all.

"You're definitely right-handed," Susan said. "Move the pencil over, and you'll see."

With my right hand, it was easy. I copied Susan's letters and they looked almost as good as her own.

"Well done," Susan said. "You've just written your name."

"That's my name?"

Jamie looked over my shoulder. "Ada," he said, nodding.

Susan took the pencil back. "And this is *Jamie*," she said. "And here's *Susan*." Then she gave Jamie the pencil. "Keep on with your work," she said. "Ada, would you put on some more coal?"

I put the coal on, but first, when Susan wasn't looking, I slid the paper into my pocket. I'd borrow a pencil the next time she was out. I'd try it again.

One afternoon near the end of November when I rode over to help Fred, he met me in the yard with a wide grin. "Come look what I've found," he said. I dismounted, tied Butter's head, unslung my crutches, and followed him to the door of the tack room. He showed me a strange-looking saddle on a stand. It had a normal seat, and one normal stirrup, but it also had two odd crooked knobs sticking up from the pommel. "It's a side-saddle," Fred said. "Must be twenty, thirty years old. Maybe more."

"So?"

"Here, I'll show you." Fred scooped the saddle up. He exchanged it for Butter's, then tossed me into it. My left leg went into the stirrup, snug beneath one of the crooks. My right leg hung down on the stirrup-less side. "Now you swing your right leg over, right here," he said. He showed me how to tuck my right thigh around the other crook, so that my right leg actually draped over the pony's left shoulder. "That's it," Fred said. "Now shove your right hip back, and get square in the saddle."

It felt very odd, but also snug and secure. As Butter had become more forward, my bad foot had become more of a problem. That I couldn't use the right stirrup was no issue, except that it tended to make me lean. But I couldn't use my right foot properly—I could thump him with it, but I couldn't keep any sort of proper contact with his side. My ankle, such as it was, didn't move that way.

"Now," Fred said, handing me a heavy leather-wrapped stick, "here's your right leg."

"My *leg*?"

"Absolutely. You haven't got one of your own legs

on the right side, see? So you hold one end of that stick and keep the other end on the pony. You'll signal him with it, just like you would with a regular leg."

Fred led us out to the field where I usually rode. "Take a bit of time to get used to it, both for him and for you." He was still grinning ear to ear. "'Ow's it feel so far?"

"Pretty good," I said. My seat could still move with Butter's walk, but my legs felt firm. "I didn't know they made saddles for cripples." I wondered where Fred had found it, whose saddle it had been.

"Nah, not for cripples," Fred said. "This is how all proper ladies used to ride. Back when, straddling a horse wasn't thought to be ladylike. But after the war, things changed—the gentry women started riding astride, and after that pretty much so did everyone."

"Which war?" Because the one we were in wasn't over.

"Last one. Twenty years back." Fred's face clouded. "England lost three million men."

"So they had lots of extra women," I said. "And lots of men's saddles for them to use."

"Suppose so." He made me go around the field, first at the walk, then at the trot. Trotting was gobs easier in the sidesaddle—I still bounced, but I couldn't really get shaken loose.

"That's enough for now," Fred said. "You can practice runnin' on your own. No jumping yet."

Never any jumping yet.

When I'd finished my work I went home by way of the tall hill above the village. Susan had drawn it on my map for me. At the top of the hill I stopped, and watched the ocean for a long time. Some days I saw ships, far off in the distance, and once or twice a fishing boat closer in. Today there was nothing but glimmering sunlight, birds circling, tiny white waves crashing against the shore. Susan said there was sand at the water's edge, and when there wasn't a war it was a lovely place to walk and look at the ocean. Just now the beach was fenced with barbed wire, and planted with mines, which were bombs in the ground, in case of invasion. We'd walk on the beach when the war was over, Susan said.

Susan didn't think I should accept the sidesaddle. She thought it was too valuable of a gift. She marched it and me over to Lady Thorton in the WVS office. "That old thing?" Lady Thorton said. "It must have been my aunt's. Mother never rode. Of course Ada may have it, or Grimes wouldn't have given it to her. Margaret doesn't want it, and neither do I."

Maggie sent me a letter from her school. Susan laid the envelope on the table one afternoon, and I traced the word I recognized on the front with my finger: Ada. I still had the paper where Susan had written my name, and I'd copied it over and over.

"Shall I read it to you?" Susan asked.

"No," I said. I opened the letter and stared at the marks on the paper inside. No matter how hard I stared, they didn't make sense. That night I tried to get Jamie to read it. "Her handwriting's all curly," he said. "I can't read that."

Still, I didn't want Susan to help me. In the end I brought it to Fred. He chewed his pipe and said Maggie wanted us to ride together when she came home for Christmas holidays.

"I won't be here for Christmas," I said. "The war will be over by then."

Fred shook his head. "I wouldn't think so," he said. "That's barely a month away. Doesn't seem to me that the war's properly started yet."

"Mam'll send for us," I said. "All the other evacuees are leaving."

Fred scratched behind his ear. "Well, we'll hope not, won't we? Don't know what I'd do without you,

I don't." He grinned at me, and to my surprise I grinned in return.

I knew I couldn't really stay. The good things here—not being shut up in the one room, for starters, and then Butter, and my crutches, and being warm even when it was cold outside. Clean clothes. Nightly baths. Three meals a day. That cup of Bovril before bedtime. The ocean seen from the top of the hill—all of these things, they were just temporary. Just until Mam came for us. I didn't dare get too used to them.

I tried to think of good things about home. I remembered Mam bringing home fish-'n'-chips on Friday nights, crisp and hot and wrapped in newspaper. I remembered that sometimes Mam sang, and laughed, and once even danced Jamie around the table. I remembered how when Jamie was little he spent his days inside with me. I remembered the crack on the ceiling that looked like a man in a pointed hat.

And even if it felt like Mam hated me, she had to love me, didn't she? She had to love me, because she was my mam, and Susan was just somebody who got stuck taking care of Jamie and me because of the war. She still said so sometimes. "I didn't ask for evacuees," she said, when Bovril puked mouse guts on the living room rug. "I don't need this," she said, shaking her head, when Jamie came home with his sweater ripped, smeared in dirt from head to toe. "I never wanted children," she said, when Butter shied at a pheasant and dumped me in the road, and ran home with my crutches tied to the saddle. Susan came out to find me, muttering, crutches in hand, and when she saw me she scowled and said it was a mercy I wasn't killed. "I never wanted children."

"I never wanted you," I said.

"I can't imagine why not," she said, snorting. "I'm so loving and kind." The wind had come up sharp and it was nearly full dark. I was shivering. When we got home Susan draped a blanket around my shoulders. "Make us some tea," she said. "I'll put up the wretched pony." She squared her shoulders and stalked into the night, and I watched her go, and wanted Mam.

I wanted Mam to be like Susan.

I didn't really trust Susan not to be like Mam.

Chapter 27

Susan took us back to see Dr. Graham. "I can't believe it's the same children," he said. Jamie was two inches taller, and I was three. We were heavier too, and I'd grown strong from riding and helping Fred. With my crutches I could walk for ages without getting tired. We didn't have impetigo, or lice, or scabs on our legs, or anything. We were the picture of health, he said. Then he took my bad foot and wriggled it. "Still nothing?" he asked Susan.

She shook her head. "I've invited her to visit for Christmas," she said. "If she comes, I hope to convince her."

"Who?" asked Jamie.

"Never you mind," Susan replied.

I was hardly paying attention. My mind always wandered into its own corner when strangers touched me. Susan tapped my shoulder. "Does this hurt?" she asked.

I shook my head. My foot hurt, it always did, but Dr. Graham wiggling it didn't make it hurt worse. I just didn't like it.

"If perhaps you could do this, every day," he said, twisting my foot as though unwringing a cloth, as though he could make it look more normal, "if she could gain some flexibility, that would only be a help for later on."

"Special shoes," I said, my mind coming back to me. "Fred said clubfoot horses had special shoes."

Dr. Graham let go of my foot. "That won't be enough at this stage," he said. "I'm convinced you'll require surgical intervention."

"Oh," I said, not having any idea what he meant.

"Still," he said, "massage might help, and certainly can do no harm."

It turned out he meant Miss Smith was going to rub and tug at my foot every night. We'd already switched to reading *Swiss Family Robinson* in the blacked-out living room after dinner, snug by the coal fire that didn't quite heat our bedrooms upstairs. Now Susan sat on one edge of the sofa, nearest the lamp, while I sat on the other and stretched my feet onto her lap. Jamie and his cat lay by the fire on the rug.

"Your foot is so cold," Susan said, the first evening. "Doesn't it feel cold?"

I nodded. We were still keeping it bandaged, but the bandage tended to get damp and my foot was nearly always freezing. "I don't mind," I said. "When it gets numb I can't feel it."

Susan looked at me, puzzled.

I said, "When it gets numb it doesn't hurt."

She winced. "You could get frostbite," she said. "That wouldn't be good for you. We need a better plan." In typical Susan fashion she set about making one. First she took one of her own thick wool stockings, which were bigger than mine and easier to slide over my inflexible ankle. Then she messed around with an old pair of slippers and a needle and thread, and pretty soon I had a sort of house shoe, with a leather bottom and knit top. It didn't keep my foot completely dry, but it helped a lot. "Hmmm," Susan said, studying the shoe. "We'll keep working."

She had her sewing machine going all the time now, three or four hours a day. She made bed jackets for soldiers from cloth the WVS gave her. She made a coat for Jamie out of an old woolen coat she said had been Becky's. She went through a pile of old clothes and ripped them apart at the seams, then washed and pressed the cloth pieces and cut and sewed them into different things entirely. "The government calls it Make Do and Mend," Susan said. "I call it how I was raised. My mother was an excellent manager."

"Does your mother hate you?" I asked.

Her face clouded. "No. She's dead, remember?"

"Did she hate you when she was alive?"

"I hope not," Susan said.

"But you said your father doesn't like you."

"No. He thinks my going to university was a bad idea."

"Did your mother think that?"

"I don't know," Susan said. "She always did whatever my father wanted." She stopped pinning pieces of cloth together. "It wasn't a good thing," she said. "It made her unhappy, but she did it anyway."

"But you didn't do what your father wanted," I said.

"It's complicated," Susan said. "At first he was pleased when I won a place at Oxford. Only later he said he didn't like the way it changed me. He thought all women should get married and I didn't do that, and—it's complicated. Only I'm not sorry I made the choices I did. If I had it to do over I'd make them again."

Susan made Jamie a pair of nice shorts to wear to church out of an old tweed skirt that had once been Becky's. She recut the jacket that had gone with the skirt and turned it into a short heavy coat I could wear when I was riding.

Since the day I broke Susan's sewing machine I'd refused to touch it, but Susan started to teach me how to sew by hand. She said it was better to learn that way first anyhow. She showed me how to sew on buttons, and I sewed the buttons onto all the bed jackets she made, and my jacket, and the flap on Jamie's shorts.

At the WVS meeting, she told the other women that I had helped her. She said so, when she came home.

One day she rummaged around in her bedroom and came out with an armful of wool yarn. She got out wooden sticks. She looped the yarn around the sticks and pretty soon had made warm hats for Jamie and me, and mufflers, and mittens to keep our hands warm.

My mittens looked like they had two thumbs apiece. Susan showed me how one thumb-part went over my thumb, and the other went over my littlest finger. She had taken very thin scraps of leather and sewed them across the palms. "They're riding mittens," she said, watching my face. "See?"

I saw. When I'd first started riding Butter I'd held the reins in my fists, but Fred insisted I do it the proper way, threading them through my third and fourth fingers and out over my thumb. In these mittens I could hold the reins right, and the leather strips would keep the yarn from wearing away.

"I made them up," Susan said. "They were all my own idea. Do you like them?"

It was one of those times when I knew the answer she wanted from me, but didn't want to give it. "They're okay," I said, and then, relenting a little, "Thank you."

"Sourpuss," she said, laughing. "Would it kill you to be grateful?"

Maybe. Who knew?

The vicar came over on a Saturday with a gang of boys and built an Anderson shelter in the back garden for us. Anderson shelters were little tin huts that were supposed to be safe from bombs. Ours didn't look safe. It looked small, and dark, and flimsy. The bottom half of it was buried in the ground, and you had to go down three steps to open the little door. Inside, there was just room for two long benches, facing each other.

Susan said we wouldn't have been able to dig the hole ourselves, not if we worked all week on it. She took drinks out to the vicar, and said so. The vicar, sweating in his shirt sleeves, said it was his pleasure. They'd been putting up Anderson shelters all over the village. It was good work for the boys.

Some of the boys were evacuees and some weren't. One was Stephen White.

He grinned and rested his shovel when I went over to him. "So you're not busy every day?" he asked.

"I am busy," I said. "I ride. I help Fred Grimes. I do things."

"I just meant, you said you were too busy to come to tea."

He used a dirty hand to push his hair away from his face, and it left a smear of mud on his cheek. Still, like me, he looked better than he had in London. His clothes were neat and clean, and he was taller.

Something about his grin made me feel I could trust him. "I wouldn't know what to do at tea," I said.

He shrugged. "Sure you do. Bet you have tea every night."

"But that colonel—"

"He's an old ducks, he is. You'd like him once you got to know him."

"How come you didn't go home with the rest of your family?" I'd been wanting to ask for ages.

Stephen looked uncomfortable. "The colonel's mostly blind," he said. "You've seen him. And he's got no family, and when I first got here he was really feeble. A bunch of the food he'd been eating had gone bad, only he's lost his sense of taste too, so he couldn't tell, and so it made him sick, and his house was just awful. Bugs everywhere, and rats, and he couldn't fix any of it.

"I cleaned the place up. The vicar's wife taught me to cook, just easy things, and she brings us food sometimes too. She's nice. And I read to the colonel, and he likes that. He's got piles of books." Stephen picked his shovel back up and started heaving dirt onto the top of the shelter. "Mum's after me to come home. I'd like to go. I miss home, I do, but if I leave, the colonel'll die. He really will. He's got no one."

Stephen looked around the muddy garden, at the house and stable and Butter's field. "Pretty nice place here."

"Yes."

"Your mam ain't come for you?"

"No. She doesn't want us."

He nodded. "Just as well. She shouldn't've shut you up like she did."

I shivered as the wind whipped higher. "It was because of my foot."

Stephen shook his head. "Foot's the same, isn't it?" he said. "And you're not shut up now. Come to tea sometime. The colonel likes having visitors."

When everyone had gone I stood just outside the door of the shelter. I didn't like it. It was dark and damp and cold; it smelled like Mam's cupboard beneath the sink. Goose bumps rose on my arms, and my stomach churned. I didn't go inside.

Susan stocked the shelter with blankets, bottles of water, candles, and matches. She said air raid sirens would go off if enemy planes were coming to bomb us. We would hear the sirens and run into the shelter, and be safe.

"What about Bovril?" Jamie asked anxiously.

Bovril could come into the shelter. Susan found an old basket with a lid on it, and put it into the shelter. If Bovril was scared, Jamie could shut him in the basket.

"He won't be scared," Jamie said. "He's *never* scared."

Butter wouldn't fit in the shelter.

Chapter 28

It was cold now and dark came early. The color had leached out of the grass in Butter's field, and he'd started to grow thin. When I showed this to Susan, she sighed. "It's all the exercise you're giving him," she said. "He used to be fat enough he could winter over on grass." She bought hay and we stacked it in one of the empty stalls. She bought a bag of oats too. Every day I took Butter three or four flakes of hay and a bucket of grain. He still lived outside. Fred said it was healthier for him, as well as being less work for us.

Back when the leaves had first started changing color on the trees, I'd been alarmed. Susan promised that it happened every year. The leaves changed color and fell off, and the trees would look dead all winter, but they wouldn't actually be dead. In spring they'd grow new green leaves again.

Susan had gotten over being surprised at all the

things we didn't know. When she showed me how to cook or sew something, she always started at the very beginning. "This is a needle. Look, it has a little hole on one end, for the thread to loop through, and a point on the other end, so it can go into cloth." Or, "Eggs have a clear part, called the white, and a yellow part, called the yolk. You break an egg by tapping it on the edge of the table, and then cracking it open with your hands. Only over the bowl, like this."

Susan said winter usually made her feel sad and gloomy, the way she was when we first came. This winter, though, she was almost too busy to be sad. She had to shop and cook and clean, and do the wash—she was particular about the wash—and sew and go to meetings. But as the days grew shorter, she did seem sad. She made an effort for us, but you could tell it was an effort. She was always tired.

I tried to be helpful. I cooked, and sewed buttons. I went with her to the shops. I learned to hem bed jackets. Meanwhile I still helped Fred twice a week, and I rode Butter every day.

On a rainy cold Wednesday afternoon Susan sat slumped in her chair. I had finished washing the lunch dishes. Jamie had gone to school. The fire was burning low, so I added coal and poked it up a little. "Thank you," Susan murmured.

She looked frail and shivery. She'd spilled a bit of potato from lunch down the front of her blouse, and not scrubbed it clean, which wasn't like her. I didn't want her staying in bed all day again. I sat down on the sofa, and I looked at her, and I said, "Maybe you could show me how to read."

She looked up disinterestedly. "Now?"

I shrugged.

She sighed. "Oh, very well." We went to the kitchen table and she got out a pencil and paper. "All the words in the world are made up of just twenty-six letters," she said. "There's a big and a little version of each."

She wrote the letters out on the paper, and named them all. Then she went through them again. Then she told me to copy them onto another piece of paper, and then she went back to her chair. I stared at the paper. I said, "This isn't reading. This is drawing."

"Writing," she corrected. "It's like buttons and hems. You've got to learn those before you can sew on the machine. You've got to know your letters before you can read."

I supposed so, but it was boring. When I said so she got up again and wrote something along the bottom of the paper.

"What's that?" I asked.

"'Ada is a curmudgeon,'" she replied.

"Ada is a curmudgeon," I copied at the end of my alphabet. It pleased me.

After that, with help from Jamie, I left Susan little notes every day. Susan is a big frog. (That one made Jamie giggle.) Butter is the best pony ever. Jamie sings like a squirrel. And then some papers I kept, because they were useful, and I could put them on the kitchen table whenever I needed to leave Susan a message. It made her happier when she knew where we were. Ada is at Fred's. Ada is riding Butter. Jamie went to the airfield.

He wasn't supposed to, but he did. They'd gotten so used to him sneaking in under the fence that they hardly bothered to scold him anymore. "Only, if they say I have to leave, I have to leave right away," Jamie told us. "If they don't say so, I can stay and talk to them." Planes fascinated him. He made friends with the pilots, and they let him sit inside the Spitfires when they were parked on the field.

Susan asked us how we usually celebrated Christmas. We didn't know what to say. Christmas was a big day at the pub, so Mam always worked. She'd get lots of tips, and usually we'd have something good to eat, fish and chips or a meat pie.

"Do you hang up your stockings?" Susan asked.

Jamie frowned. "What for?"

We'd heard of Father Christmas—it was something other children talked about—but we didn't get visits from him.

I said, "What do you usually do?"

Her face went soft, remembering. "The Christmases when Becky was alive we'd have a big dinner with some of our friends," she said. "Roast goose, or turkey. In the morning we'd exchange presents—we always had a little tree, and we'd decorate the windowsills with holly—and then we'd have something wonderful for breakfast, hot sticky buns and bacon and coffee, and then we'd just laze around until it was time to start making dinner. On Boxing Day Becky would go hunting.

"When I was little, my family all went to midnight services on Christmas Eve. My father would preach. The church always looked beautiful in the cold candlelight. Then I'd go to sleep—such a short sleep!—and wake up to my stocking filled with little presents at the foot of my bed. The bigger gifts were downstairs, under the tree. Mother cooked a huge meal, and all the aunts and uncles and cousins came . . ." Her voice trailed away. "We'll do something nice," she said, "for your first Christmas here."

"Can Mam come?" Jamie asked.

Susan put her hand on his head. "I hope she will,"

she said. "I've invited her, but I haven't gotten a reply."

"I'll write to her," Jamie said.

"You don't have to," I told him. It seemed risky. If we reminded Mam that we were here, would she come and get us?

"We need to talk to her about your foot," Susan said.

"Well, I'm not writing," I said. I had memorized the alphabet, and was starting to understand how the letters should sound, so that I could read even words I hadn't seen before. I could write, a bit. But not to Mam.

"You don't have to," Susan said, her arm around me.

The shops filled with the most amazing things: oranges and nuts and all sorts of candy and toys. Susan said people were determined to have a happy Christmas despite the war. She herself ordered a goose, since Jamie and I had never had one, and then she invited some of the pilots from the airfield to come eat it with us, because the goose was too big for the three of us alone. I invited Fred, but he said he always went to his brother's house and he didn't like to break tradition. "But thank you kindly," he added.

So I invited Maggie.

It seemed right to me that if Jamie got to have pilots, I should have a friend to dinner too. Besides Fred, and maybe Stephen, Maggie was the only friend I had.

She came back from her school the week before Christmas. We rode together up the big hill, where the wind was blowing hard and we could see down to the barricaded beach. Maggie was different, stiffer and more standoffish than she'd been the day I rode her home. She looked elegant on her pony, with her leather gloves and her little velvet cap.

I put my hand up to shield my eyes. Riding up the hill had been my idea. "I always check for spies when I'm up here," I said. "We're supposed to, you know." We were told so by the government men on the radio. Nazi spies could be dressed as nurses, or nuns, or anything.

"I know," Maggie said crossly. "I'm not stupid." Then she added, "Why didn't you write back to me? I asked you to."

I hadn't known she'd asked me. Fred hadn't read me that part of her letter. And while I'd had another couple of goes at reading it, Maggie's handwriting was curly with the letters run together. I couldn't make out the words.

I was ashamed to admit this. "I've been very busy," I said.

She flashed me a look of hurt and anger. I understood, suddenly, that she'd been waiting for me to write back, waiting and hoping for a letter. I didn't know she felt that way about me.

I took a deep breath. "I'm just now learning to write," I said. "And read. So I couldn't write back yet. I'm sorry. Next time I'll try."

Instead of looking horrified by my ignorance, she looked mollified. (Susan taught me that word, and I loved it. *Mollified.* Sometimes when Jamie was cross, he had to be mollified.) "I didn't think of that," she said. "I thought you just weren't interested. But wouldn't Miss Smith have helped you? She would have written down what you wanted to say."

She would have, if I'd asked. "I didn't want to ask her. I don't like her helping me."

"Why ever not?"

"I don't want to get used to her," I said. "She's just someone we have to stay with for a little while. She's not, you know, actually real."

Maggie looked me up and down. "She seems real to me," she said. "I saw you the day you got off that train. You looked like you'd already been through a war. Then you looked better the day you helped me. And now! Sidesaddle on a pony, and fancy clothes, and not so skinny your bones show. Your eyes are different too. Before, you looked scared to death."

I didn't want to talk about it. There weren't any spies in view, nor any ships, and Butter was tired of standing in the wind. "Race you to the village," I said.

Chapter 29

Maggie won, but not by much, and I stayed in the saddle the whole time even though Butter galloped faster than he'd ever gone before. We followed Maggie's pony over two fallen logs—little soaring jumps, my first. By the time we pulled up on the outskirts of town, both ponies blowing hard, Maggie's hair had come loose from its plait and her cheeks were bright red. She was laughing. She'd forgotten I ever looked scared.

I knew Susan wasn't real. Or, if she was a tiny bit real, sometimes, at the very best she was only temporary. She'd be done with us once the war was over, or whenever Mam changed her mind.

Maggie couldn't come for Christmas dinner. She said she wished she could, but her brother was expected home from aviation training, and her father was coming from wherever he was doing secret war work, and they were all having their traditional Christmas. So of course she had to stay home. "It'll be a miserable day," she said. "Mum will be trying not to blubber over Jonathan, so she'll be snippy with everyone. Dad's wound up about Hitler and won't talk about anything but the war, especially since there's no hunting, and Mum *hates* talking about the war. The cook quit to work in a factory and the housekeeper's an awful cook, and we've not got but one maid left, and no footmen in the house at all. So I'll be scrubbing on Christmas Eve and Mum will be trying to help cook, and we'll sit down in this big fancy room with cobwebs in the corners and eat horrible food and pretend to be cheerful and nothing, *nothing* will be like it used to.

"People keep saying it isn't really a war," she said. "Hardly anybody's being bombed, hardly anybody's fighting. It feels like a war to me. A war right in my family." She gave me a sideways look. "You're probably happy," she said.

"I'm not happy because you're miserable," I shot back.

She shook her head. "Oh, of course not. Come on." We were riding again, but this time we took a path Maggie chose, through woods down to the beach. We had to stay on the far side of the barbed wire, but we followed the road along the beach and watched the waves crash against the shore. It amazed me, how different the ocean could look from day to day.

Susan took an ax and made us go with her out into somebody's field and cut down a little tree. It was not a tree that went dead in the winter. It had little green spikes on its branches instead of leaves and Susan called it an evergreen.

It was snowing, and the air was wet and cold. "What for?" I asked. Susan and Jamie lugged the tree home while I walked with my crutches beside them.

"Christmas trees," Susan said, "remind us that God is like an evergreen tree—even in winter, never dead."

"But you said the other trees weren't dead either," Jamie pointed out.

"Well, no, they're not," Susan said. "But they look dead. And Christmas trees are a nice tradition. Green in the midst of winter, light in the midst of darkness—it's all metaphors for God."

I ignored the word *metaphor,* but asked, "What's Christmas got to do with God?"

Well. You would think I'd said something really odd. Susan gaped at me, mouth open, fishlike, and when she finally closed her mouth she sputtered,

"Haven't you been learning anything going to church?"

I shrugged. Church was hard to follow. Sometimes the stories made sense, but mostly they didn't, and although the vicar seemed nice, I almost never actually listened to him. I might have liked the songs if I could have read them fast enough to actually sing.

It turned out Christmas was Jesus's birthday. Jesus was the man hanging on the cross up in the front of the church—I already knew that part. So, easy enough. But then Jamie asked, "How did they *know*? When Jesus's birthday was?"

Susan said, "Well. I don't suppose they did know. Not absolutely."

Jamie nodded. "Like Ada and me."

"Right," Susan said. "But we've got your pretend birthdays on your identity cards, so we'll celebrate your birthdays on those days. Christmas is like that."

Jamie said, "Was Christmas the birthday on Jesus's identity card?"

"You stupid," I said. "Jesus wasn't in a war."

"Don't call him stupid," Susan said.

"It was a stupid thing to say."

"Saying something stupid doesn't make you stupid," Susan said. "Luckily for all of us."

We took the tree into the house and set it up in the corner of the living room. Susan put a string of little electric lights in its branches. She went into Becky's room upstairs and came out with a big box. She looked inside, blinked back tears, and shut the box again.

"Let's make our own ornaments," she said. "Wouldn't you like that?"

How would I know? I could tell she wanted me to like it, and I didn't want her to cry. It made me nervous when she cried. "Yes?" I said.

"Oh, Ada." She gave me a hug with her free arm. I took a deep breath, and didn't pull away. "These are the ornaments Becky and I put on our trees together. I'm not ready to have them out again."

"Okay," I said.

"Okay?" she asked. "Really?"

I didn't know what to say. Somehow Christmas was making me feel jumpy inside. All this talk about being together and being happy and celebrating—it felt threatening. Like I shouldn't be part of it. Like I wasn't allowed. And Susan *wanted* me to be happy, which was scarier still.

Ornaments were little pretty things you hung on a Christmas tree. Susan got out colored paper, and scissors, and glue. She showed us how to make snow-flakes and stars. I worked hard to make mine as good as hers. Jamie cut his paper quick into ragged shapes. We hung them all up, ragged and careful both, and the tree did look pretty in the corner of the room. Bovril thought so too. He lay under it during the day, batting the lowest ornaments with his paws. Jamie wadded up some of the leftover paper, and in the evenings tossed it back and forth across the floor for Bovril to pounce upon.

I hated sharing my bed with a cat. Sometimes I woke with a tail in my face and there always seemed to be hair in the sheets. Jamie insisted he could only sleep if Bovril was tucked up with him, and Bovril, drat him, seemed to feel the same way.

It snowed again. When I rode Butter over to Maggie's, snow balled up under his feet, and clumped in the bottom of his tail. The whole world was white and sparkling. Snow in London didn't stay white for long.

Maggie'd been helping Fred every day since she'd come home, and on the days when I was there we all worked together. Fred had started me properly jumping now, little jumps, but not today because the snow was too deep.

"You know you're supposed to get Susan a Christmas present," Maggie said as we measured oats in the feed room.

"Why?" I asked. I'd heard about presents. I didn't get them. I didn't need to give them. I said so.

Maggie rolled her eyes at me. "Of course you'll be getting presents," she said. "Susan is nice to you. Not like some."

I nodded. Some of the evacuees, those that were left, weren't treated very kindly. Not because of anything to do with them, but because they'd been put with mean old hags who wouldn't have welcomed Jesus himself. At least that's what Jamie said. He talked to the other evacuees at school, and they were envious, they were, that they hadn't been chosen last.

"So," Maggie said, "you should get her something. It's only right."

"I haven't got any money. Not any at all."

"Don't you get pocket money?"

"No. Do you?"

"Oh," Maggie said. She chewed her bottom lip

while she thought. "Well, you could find some job to do, and earn something. I suppose. Or you could make her something. She'd like that. My mum always likes it when I make her something."

It was an interesting idea. I thought about it as I started home. Susan had been teaching me to knit so that I could knit for the soldiers, but so far the only thing I'd made had been a washcloth. It was a hideous washcloth, wider on one end than the other, with loopy stitches that looked nothing like Susan's. Susan claimed it didn't matter, because soldiers would be glad to have a washcloth no matter what it looked like. She also said knitting was like writing, or riding, or anything else: You got better the more you worked at it.

I could work at it, if I hurried. I turned Butter in the road, and, despite his protests, made him go back through the snow to Maggie's house. Fred looked surprised to see me. "Trouble?" he asked.

"I need some wool," I said.

Chapter 30

"Aye," Fred said, nodding, as though girls rode to him through snowstorms all the time, needing wool. He disappeared into the stables, and I heard him clop up the stairs to the rooms in the loft where he lived. He came down carrying a cloth bag printed in bright flowers. "It's the missus's knitting bag," he said, thrusting it at me. "It's full of wool. All sorts. You can have it."

I didn't know he had a missus. "Aye," he said, in response to my unspoken question. "She's been dead five years. Was nurse to Miss Margaret and Master Jonathan, and before that to their mother and her brothers."

I squashed the bulky bag beneath my jacket to keep it out of the snow. Butter tossed his head, restless, and I let him turn for home.

"Wait." Fred grabbed Butter's bridle. "When

someone gives you a present," he said, with a gentle smile, "you say 'Thank you.'"

Susan had taught me that, but I'd been so busy thinking about the wool the bag contained that I'd forgotten. "Thank you, Fred," I said. "Thank you very much. I wish I could say thank you to your missus too."

"Ah, well." He shook his head. "Happen she'd be glad I found her things a good home. You're very welcome, child."

It was Thursday already and Christmas was Monday, so I didn't have much time. When I got home I dumped the bag onto my bed. There were five sets of knitting needles, from thick to thin, and a handful of smaller thin sticks that were pointed on both ends. There were all sorts of oddments of wool, rolled into balls, and there were six balls of fine, white wool.

The white wool would be best. I had plenty of it. I cast on and started to work.

I expected Susan to be suspicious when I spent the whole afternoon in my cold bedroom, and she was. "What are you up to?" she asked at dinner.

I ran through my options in my head. I wasn't

sleeping. I wasn't taking a bath. I couldn't be listening to the radio. Stalling while I searched for a plausible excuse, I said, "Nothing."

To my surprise, she grinned. "Oh, really? I'll make a bargain with you. You can have a few hours of nothing time upstairs anytime the rest of this week you like, as long as you give me the same amount of nothing time downstairs. You shout before you come down, and wait until I tell you okay. Deal?"

I could only nod. In the days to come I could sometimes hear the whirr of her sewing machine while I knit upstairs. I took a hot water bottle with me and put a blanket around my shoulders, and I knit white wool and oddments all the next two days. Wretched Bovril started wanting to sit in my lap on top of the water bottle, until I threw him out and shut the door.

The day before Christmas was a Sunday. When Jamie and I got up we dressed in the clothes Susan insisted we save for Sundays, Jamie in his white shirt and tweed shorts and good dark socks, me in the red dress Maggie had given me. We went down to breakfast and Susan shook her head. "Sorry, forgot. Go put your regular things on for the day. We're going to church at night. All of us, even me. It's Christmas Eve."

Because it was Christmas Eve we had bacon at

breakfast. During the day I helped make biscuits. Jamie roasted chestnuts for the goose's dressing. Susan put the radio on, and sang along to the Christmas music.

Midafternoon she made us bathe. She brushed my hair downstairs by the fire until it was dry, and braided it in two plaits instead of one. We ate supper, and then she told Jamie to go upstairs and put on his church clothes. She told me to sit still. "I have a surprise."

She put a big box wrapped in paper onto my lap. Inside was a dress made of soft dark green fabric. It had puffed sleeves and a round collar, and it gathered at the waist before billowing out into a long, full skirt.

It was so beautiful I couldn't touch it. I just stared.

"Come," Susan said. "Let's see if it fits."

I held perfectly still while she took off my sweater and blouse, and settled the green dress over my head. "Step out of your skirt," Susan said, and I did. She buttoned the dress and stepped back. "There," she said, smiling, her eyes soft and warm. "It's perfect. Ada. You're beautiful."

She was lying. She was lying, and I couldn't bear it. I heard Mam's voice shrieking in my head. "*You ugly piece of rubbish! Filth and trash! No one wants you, with that ugly foot!*" My hands started to shake. Rubbish. Filth. Trash. I could wear Maggie's discards, or plain clothes from the shops, but not this, not this beautiful dress. I could listen to Susan say she never wanted children all day long. I couldn't bear to hear her call me beautiful.

"What's the matter?" Susan asked, perplexed. "It's a Christmas present. I made it for you. Bottle green velvet, just like I said."

Bottle green velvet. "I can't wear this," I said. I pulled at the bodice, fumbling for the buttons. "I can't wear it. I can't."

"Ada." Susan grabbed my hands. She pulled me to the sofa and set me down hard beside her, still restraining me. "*Ada*. What would you say to Jamie, if I gave him something nice and he said he couldn't have it? Think. What would you say?"

Tears were running down my face now. I started to panic. I fought Susan's grasp. "I'm not Jamie!" I said. "I'm different, I've got the ugly foot, I'm—" My throat closed over the word *rubbish*.

"Ada. Ada." I felt I could hardly hear Susan's voice. A scream built up from somewhere inside me, came roaring out in an ocean of sound. Scream after scream—Jamie running half-dressed down the stairs, Susan pinning down my arms, holding me against her, holding me tight. Waves of panic hit me, over and over, turning me and tossing me until I thought I'd drown.

Chapter 31

We didn't go to church. We ended up on the floor in front of the fire, wrapped in blankets Jamie dragged down the stairs. All of us. I don't know how long I screamed and flailed. I don't know how long Susan restrained me. I kicked her and scratched her and probably would have bitten her, but she held on. I don't know what Jamie did, other than bring down the blankets. Susan wrapped me in one, rolled me up tight, and the panic started to ease. "That's it," Susan croaked. "Shh. Shh. You're okay."

I was not okay. I would never be okay. But I was too exhausted to scream anymore.

When I woke, the first rays of winter sunlight were coming through the window onto the little Christmas tree. The coal embers shone dully beneath a layer of ashes. Jamie slept wrapped in a blanket with Bovril's face peeping out beneath his chin. Susan snored gently. One of her arms was flung up, under her ear; the other still rested across me. Her hair had come out of its bun and was sticking out in all directions. She had a long red furrow down one cheek from where I'd scratched her, and her blouse—her best blouse—had a rip at the shoulder and a button hanging by a thread. She looked like she'd been in a war.

I was so completely wound in a gray blanket that I could only move my head. I turned it from side to side, looking first at Jamie, then at Susan, then at the little Christmas tree. Susan would be angry when she woke. She would be furious, because I'd screamed about the dress, because I hadn't been grateful, because I'd messed up her plans. We hadn't gone to church because of me.

My stomach worked itself into a knot. She would be angry. She would hit—no. She wouldn't hit me. She hadn't, at least not so far. She hadn't hit me once the night before, not even when I'd hurt her. She'd wrapped me up and held me tight.

I didn't know what to do. Susan was temporary. My foot was permanent. I lay in the weak sunshine and wanted to weep instead of scream. But I almost never cried. What was wrong with me now?

Jamie stirred. He opened his eyes and *smiled*— smiled his beautiful smile. All of my life I would remember the sweetness of that smile. "Good morning, Ada," Jamie said. "Merry Christmas."

I didn't know what Susan had said or done to Jamie before he fell asleep, but he woke as though sleeping on the living room floor was perfectly ordinary. He sat up, rubbed Bovril's belly, then put the cat outside to do his business and added coal to the fire.

The rattle of the coal scuttle woke Susan. I watched her carefully as she opened her eyes and came to an awareness of where she was. She saw me, and she smiled too.

Smiled.

"Good morning, Ada," she said. "Merry Christmas."

I wanted to bury my head in my blankets and weep and scream, but I didn't. Instead I said, "I can't get up. I can't move my arms."

She sat up and untangled me. "I wasn't trying to trap you," she said. "It seemed to soothe you, to be bundled like that."

"I know," I said. "It did." I pointed to the rip on her blouse.

"It's in a seam," she said. "I can fix it." She brushed my loose hair back from my face. "Would you like some breakfast?"

We got up and went upstairs and washed our faces and used the loo. At Susan's suggestion we took off our good clothes and put on our pajamas and dressing gowns. When we came back down the stairs, there was a pile of brightly wrapped packages under the tree.

Presents.

"Looks like Santa Claus has been here," Susan said gaily.

Seemed odd that Santa Claus would stay away all night, but come while we were changing our clothes. I opened my mouth to say so, but saw Jamie's glowing face in time and shut up fast.

Jamie's eyes were lit with joy. "He really did come! To us! He did!" he said. "Even though Ada was bad." He gave me a quick guilty look. "I mean—"

"It's okay," I said, slipping my arm around his shoulders. "I *was* bad." I wondered if the presents were all for Jamie. Could any possibly be for me?

"Not bad," Susan said. She helped me down the last few steps. "Not bad, Ada. Sad. Angry. Frightened. Not bad."

Sad, angry, frightened *were* bad. It was not okay to be any of those. I couldn't say so, though, not on that gentle morning.

I had the gifts I'd made stuffed into the pockets of my dressing gown. I didn't have any paper to wrap them. I wasn't sure what to do.

"Breakfast," Susan said. She'd put the kettle on

for tea, and started a pan full of sizzling sausages. She fried us each an egg. On the table, laid across our plates, were two of our stockings, one each. They were stuffed full and knobbly. I poked mine. "You should have hung those up last night," she said. "But I see Santa found them anyway. Have a look inside while I finish cooking."

An orange. A handful of walnuts. Boiled sweets. Two long hair ribbons, one green and one blue. In the toe, a shilling.

Jamie had the same, except he had a whistle instead of hair ribbons, and an India rubber ball.

Shiny bright girls, with ribbons in their hair. I wanted to weep all over again. I wanted to scream.

What was wrong with me?

I couldn't mess up Jamie's Christmas. I stroked the satin ribbons and went away in my head. I was on Butter, up on the hill, galloping, galloping—

"Ada." Susan touched my shoulder. "Come back."

Fried sausages on my plate. A fried egg, its yolk as bright as the sun. Toast, and strong hot tea. Jamie blew his whistle—a piercing shriek. "Save that for outside," Susan said, ruffling his hair.

After breakfast we opened our presents. Jamie got a toy motorcar and a set of building blocks. I got a new halter for Butter, and a pad of paper and a set of colored pencils. We each got a book. Mine was called *Alice in Wonderland*. Jamie's was *Peter Pan*.

Susan didn't get anything from Santa Claus. She told Jamie grown-ups didn't. But I pulled my gifts from my pocket. For Jamie I had a scarf made of all the oddments of yarn, different colors and kinds, in stripes. He looked at it and frowned. "I like the scarf Susan made me better," he said. Susan poked him and he said, "Thank you," which kept me from smacking him.

Then I gave Susan her scarf, knit from the white wool. I'd made hers last of all my gifts, so it would be the best, because I really did get better at knitting the more I did it.

Susan unfolded it against her knee. "Ada, it's beautiful. This is what you've been doing?"

"I got the wool from Fred," I said quickly, so she'd know I hadn't stolen it.

She hugged me. "I love it. I'll wear it every day."

I shrugged her away. It was too much, all this emotion. I wanted to get away. She seemed to understand even that. "Put your jods on and run out to see your pony," she said. "Jamie'll help me clear up, and we'll get started on dinner."

Jamie's three pilots came midafternoon. They wore their best uniforms and identical polite smiles. They gave Susan a bottle of wine, a box of chocolates, and a potted plant. Susan told them she felt like she was getting the gifts of the Magi, and they laughed.

The house smelled like roast goose. The fireplace crackled. The sun was setting already, and the living room looked warm and bright even with the blackouts up. The pilots sat awkwardly on the sofa, all in a row, but then Jamie started cutting up, running his new car over their knees and grinning and acting silly, and pretty soon one of the pilots was on the floor playing with Jamie, making towers with the building blocks and smashing into them with the car, and Susan gave the other two pilots glasses of wine and everyone seemed much more relaxed.

I wasn't relaxed. I was wearing the green dress.

I'd put it on when I came in from seeing Butter, because I knew it would please Susan, and it did. She brushed my hair and let it hang loose, tying my new green ribbon around my head. "That's an Alice ribbon," she said. "The girl in your book, Alice, she wears her hair like that."

I felt like an imposter. It was worse than when I tried to talk like Maggie. Here I was, looking like Maggie. Looking like a shiny bright girl with hair ribbons. Looking like a girl with a family that loved her.

Jamie squeezed my arm. "You look nice," he whispered, scanning my face anxiously.

I took a deep breath. I did have family that loved me. Jamie loved me.

Susan called us to dinner. She'd put Christmas crackers by everyone's plate. I'd never seen them before. They were tubes of paper; when you pulled the ends apart, they made a cracking noise and paper crowns and little toys fell out of them. We all wore our paper crowns to dinner. The pilots and Susan and Jamie laughed and talked, and I ate goose and tried to keep my insides still.

"That's a pretty dress," one of the pilots said to me.

I felt prickly all over, like my skin was too tight for my body, but I wasn't going to let myself lose control again. "Thank you," I said. "It's new." It was kind of him to mention my dress instead of my bad foot. I told myself that, over and over, and kept still.

When they left, Susan sat me on the sofa beside her. "That was hard for you," she said. I nodded. She pulled me against her, tight, the way she had the night before except that I wasn't screaming. "Put the radio on, Jamie," she said. "Ada, let's see to your foot." I sighed and arranged myself on the sofa, my bad foot in her lap. She pulled off my stocking and started rubbing and twisting it, the way she did every night. We were, she said, making a very small bit of progress.

"Where's our book?" Jamie said, and went to fetch it. We were halfway through reading *Swiss Family Robinson* for the second time. I understood the story better now, but I still didn't like it. The family landed on the perfect island, where everything they needed was right in front of them. Susan pointed out that they had to work together to put the good things to use. Jamie just liked the adventures.

"Not that," I said. "Read mine." I made Jamie fetch *Alice in Wonderland*. Between Alice's hair ribbon and the word *wonderland*, I doubted I'd like it, but it was better than more Family Robinson.

It *was* better. Alice chased after a rabbit who was wearing clothes and a pocket watch. He went down his hole just like the rabbits I saw when I was out on Butter, but she went after him, and fell into a place she didn't belong, a place where absolutely nothing made sense to her.

It was us, I thought. Jamie and me. We had fallen down a rabbit hole, fallen into Susan's house, and nothing made sense, not at all, not anymore.

Chapter 32

In January rationing began. It was a way of sharing out what food there was so that rich people, like Susan, couldn't go hogging it and leaving poor people to starve. Rationing meant there might not be any butter or meat in the shops, and if there was you'd better get in the queue for it fast before it sold out. We all had ration books that said how much food we were allowed.

It made Jamie nervous. Me too. Susan had always given us plenty of food, but we knew that was because she was rich, no matter what she said. I'd gotten used to eating regular.

We tried eating less. The first time Jamie asked to be excused before he finished his dinner Susan felt his forehead. "Are you sick?" she asked. He shook his head. "Then eat. I know you can't be full."

"I'll save it for tomorrow," he said.

I pushed my plate away. "Me too."

Susan told us firmly that we were not to save our dinners. She said rationing meant we would have to eat different kinds of food, more vegetables, less meat, less butter and sweets. It did not mean there would not be enough food. There would always be enough food. She would personally see that we always had enough to eat.

"Even if you have to get a job?" I asked her.

"Yes," she said firmly. "Even if I have to char."

Chars were the lowliest kind of cleaning lady. Some of the older girls on our lane back home were chars.

"Why?" I asked.

She looked at me, blank.

"Why? You didn't want us. You don't even like us."

Jamie held perfectly still. Susan sipped her tea, the way she always did when she was stalling. "Of course I like you," she said. "Don't I act as though I like you?"

I shrugged.

"I never wanted children," she continued, "because you can't have children without being married, and I never wanted to be married. When I shared this home with Becky, that was the happiest I had ever been. I wouldn't have traded that for anything, not even children.

"I was so sad the day you came—but it wasn't about you. I was just sad. I didn't think I could take good care of you. I didn't think I could take care of any children."

"And you didn't want to," I said. "Especially us."

Susan said, "Ada, what's this about really? The better you get, the worse you seem."

I shrugged again. It was scary, how angry I felt inside. At Susan, for being temporary. At Mam, for not caring about us. At Fred, for wearing the scarf I had knit him from his wife's wool every day, as though it was something special, when I could see myself how I'd dropped some stitches and picked up others, so that the scarf was full of holes.

At Maggie, for loaning me her copy of *Alice's Adventures Through the Looking Glass* when I told her how much I liked *Alice in Wonderland.* As though books were something you could just give out like yesterday's newspapers. As though I would be able to sit down and read it as easily as she would. As though the letter I sent her when she went back to school, which took me hours and was full of scratches and misspellings, was anything at all like her letter back to me, written in ink with the curvy handwriting.

At the war, for taking us away from Mam before she realized she loved us.

At myself, for being so glad to go.

"Ada." Susan spoke slowly and clearly. "Right now

you are here. I am not sending you or Jamie anywhere. You will both stay here. I will take care of you.
You will have enough to eat. You are learning to read
and write, and next year you will go to school. We will
get your mother's permission, and as soon as we do,
we will get the operation to fix your foot. All will be
well. Relax."

When she started to speak I almost went away, to
the place in my head where I didn't feel anything. But
Susan tapped my arm, keeping me with her, and she
put her hand lightly around my wrist while she spoke.
I pulled my hand away, but I stayed where I could
hear her. That's how I heard the words "an operation
to fix your foot."

Fix my foot? What on earth did she mean?

Three days later I rode Butter to the top of the hill.
I halted where we could see the sea, dark and vio-
lent and thrashing, where the wind whipped Butter's
mane against my bad foot, held as it was by the crook
of the sidesaddle. The wind blew the wisps of hair
around my face and made tears come to my eyes, and
I could feel its coldness even through my warm coat
and hat and mittens.

No boats anywhere. No signs of spies. New towers
built near the beach, and more barbed wire, and what

looked like soldiers marching along the ocean's edge. Our soldiers—if it were the Germans invading, the church bells would have rung.

I rode slowly down the hill, through the village. The butcher standing in his shop door nodded his head to me. One of the women I passed smiled. Another waved. They saw me ride by every day. If they thought I should be kept locked up, at least they didn't say so. They didn't look disgusted by me.

At home I untacked Butter and rubbed him dry. I fed him and combed out his tangled mane. I cleaned the saddle and bridle and put them neatly away. I took my time.

Then I went into the house, where Susan was, and asked, "What does the word *operation* mean?"

Chapter 33

Susan took me back to see Dr. Graham so he could explain. He did not reexamine my foot. We sat in his office, all three of us, and he talked, and I listened.

"First of all," he said, "understand that we can't proceed without your mother's permission. At this point it would have to be considered elective surgery, and that's why we've been waiting for her approval." He glanced up at Susan. "You haven't gotten it?" She shook her head.

"Well, I have been reading up on the procedure," Dr. Graham said. "It wouldn't be me who would do the surgery, we'd have to send you to a specialist. I've written to one that I think would be best. He does say that you won't ever have a normal foot. Please understand that. You could have if treatment had started early enough, but you can't now. You won't get a normally functioning ankle. But we could hope for a foot that looked normally positioned, that you could walk on with the plantar surface down." He looked at me and added, "That means the bottom. What should be the bottom of your foot would be the part touching the ground."

I thought about this. "Would it hurt?" I asked.

"You would be sleeping during the surgery," he said. "We would give you special medicine to make you stay asleep, and you wouldn't feel anything then. Afterward, yes, it would probably hurt. You'd need to stay in hospital for quite a long time too—probably several months. Your foot would be kept in plaster casts."

"Would I be able to wear shoes?"

His eyes smiled, even though his mouth did not. "Yes," he said. "When everything was healed, you would."

I thought of something else. "Who pays for it?" I asked. It cost a pile of money to stay in hospital.

Susan and the doctor exchanged glances. "We'll deal with that problem when we come to it," Dr. Graham said. "I'm sure there are charities we could get involved."

Susan and I walked home silently through the blustery freezing wind.

"What are you thinking?" she finally asked.

"He said if I'd started treatment early, I could have had a normal foot."

"Yes," Susan said. "Most babies born with clubfeet have them fixed right away."

"All the way fixed?"

Susan put her hand on my shoulder. "Yes. All the way."

I could have always lived outside the one room. I could have been like Jamie, running fast. I said, "I thought you kept writing to Mam because you wanted to get rid of us."

Susan said, "No wonder you were angry."

I felt fragile, not the way I had when I'd exploded on Christmas Eve, but the way I'd felt the next morning, when the only thing that kept me together was Jamie's smile. Jamie's and Susan's smiles.

At home I sat at the table while Susan put the kettle on. "Do you want to go ride?" she asked. I shook my head. I drank the tea she put in front of me. I pulled my plait over my shoulder and studied the blue ribbon at the end of it. Then I pulled off the slipper shoe Susan had made, and pulled off my stocking, and looked at my foot. The awkward U-shaped ankle. The tiny toes that curled up, not down. The rough calluses where my skin had torn open and then healed, over and over again.

Susan said, "It's not your fault."

I said, "I always thought it was. I thought I'd done something wrong."

"I know," Susan said.

"It's disgusting," I said.

Susan said, "I never thought so."

I searched her face to see if it was a lie. She looked at me steadily. She said, "If you feel very angry, go outside and throw something."

I didn't feel angry. I felt sad. So sad I could get lost in the sadness. But when I finished my tea, I got out paper and a pencil, and in my very best handwriting, wrote a letter.

Dear Mam, it said, *please let them fix me.*

Chapter 34

I waited for a reply.

Twice a day the postman dropped letters through the slot on the front door. Twice a day I went to look. Susan said it would take at least two days for the letter to get to London, and two days for an answer to come back to us, but ten days passed and still there was nothing.

"I bet they aren't delivering letters in London," Jamie said. "Because of the war." I could tell by the look on Susan's face she didn't think that was true.

On the twelfth day a letter I recognized fell at my feet. My own. *Return to sender* was scrawled across it. *No longer at this address.*

"She's moved," Susan said, turning the unopened envelope over in her hands. "She lives somewhere else now."

Susan said perhaps Mam had a new job and had moved to be closer to it. She said perhaps the government had requisitioned our flat. She said there were a number of reasons that Mam might have moved that didn't mean she'd abandoned us, and she, Susan, would make inquiries through the WVS. Someone in London was bound to know where Mam had gone.

"What happens to us?" Jamie asked, wide-eyed.

"You stay with me," Susan said, "just like you do now. Your mam knows where you are. She knows you're safe."

"What happens when the war's over?"

Susan took a deep breath. "Your mam will come and get you."

"What if she doesn't?" Jamie insisted.

"Don't worry," Susan said. "I'll make sure someone always takes care of you."

"I'll take care of him," I said, suddenly furious. "I took care of him before, not Mam." I hated—I hated—*oh*. Even in my head I still couldn't say I hated Mam. Even now. If I could get my foot fixed, maybe she'd be different. Maybe she'd love me. Maybe she would.

"You did a good job taking care of Jamie," Susan said. "But it was a big job, and you shouldn't have had to do it. So now you can relax. I can take care of you. You don't have to fight so hard."

She couldn't take care of me. She talked about fixing my foot, but she couldn't do it, not really. It was all just lies. And I wanted my foot fixed so badly. I was tired of it hurting. I wanted to be like a normal person. I wanted to walk without crutches, and I wanted to go to school, and I wanted to wear shoes on both feet. I never wanted to be locked up again.

I hated crying, but I couldn't help it. I sat on the sofa and sobbed. Susan held me to her. "I know," she said. "I'm so sorry. I know." She stroked my hair. "If it was emergency surgery," she said, "if you broke your leg or if your life was in danger, I could give permission for that. But this is a big operation, and it is elective, you can survive without it. I can't give permission. I've asked the WVS and I've consulted a lawyer, and without your mam's permission we can't have it done. I'm so sorry. We'll keep looking for her. We'll find her."

"I don't want to just *survive*," I said.

"I know," Susan said. "So you'll have to figure out how to make that happen, without fixing your foot.

"It's hard," she said, "but that's the truth."

The winter turned fierce. Snow drifted over the fields and made it impossible for Butter to climb our hill. Even the ride to Fred's was so wretchedly cold I dreaded it. I went every day now, for afternoon feed, because the winter work was too much for Fred. He didn't watch me ride. It was far too cold for that. I put Butter in a stall and did chores with Fred as fast as possible, and then rode home. Water froze in the troughs. The horses ate mountains of hay.

"It's getting to be too much for you," Susan said, when I came home with my toes and fingers numb, shivering so hard I couldn't stop. "If Fred can't manage, Lady Thorton will have to hire someone to help him, war or no war."

"It's not too much for me," I said. "I promise."

Susan insisted I would attend the village school next year. She borrowed all sorts of books from the town library and made me read them. If I couldn't read a word, I was supposed to ask her what it meant. The more I read, the less I had to ask. She started me on math and history too.

Our days went like this. Susan woke us in the dark and cold. We washed up and dressed as quickly as we could. Downstairs, Jamie tended the fire in the living room while Susan worked the range. I went out to give Butter hay. After breakfast Jamie washed the dishes by himself while Susan and I took the blackouts down. Then we had housework, reading, and sewing. Jamie played with Bovril on the rug. Lunch, school for Jamie, shopping for Susan, me helping Fred. More chores, then dinner. Susan would read out loud while she massaged my bad foot, and then we went to sleep under the mountain of blankets Susan had piled on our bed.

Susan looked horrified when the first chilblains appeared on my bad foot. I shrugged. "I always get them," I said. She shook her head at me and consulted Fred. He found a piece of stout leather meant for tack repair, and together he and Susan designed a sort of boot. I stepped my bad foot into it and buttoned it up the side. It was loose, so I could wear extra stockings, and Fred oiled it until it stayed dry even in wet mushy snow. That kept the chilblains from getting worse. They didn't heal, however, which distressed Susan.

"I don't know why," I said. "They're not bad."

"They must hurt," she said. I shrugged. They did, and the itching sometimes kept me awake nights, but I couldn't do anything about it.

"My foot always hurts," I said. "I always get chilblains in winter." Usually I got them on my hands as well.

"Next winter," Susan said, "we'll stop them before they get started. There must be some way."

I looked at her. "Will I be here next winter?"

She said, "It's starting to look that way. The war's not going anywhere." She bought goose grease in the village and rubbed it on my sores.

Stephen's colonel invited me for tea again and this time I went. The winter was so bleak I was glad to have something different to do, and, anyway, I wasn't as afraid of things as I had been.

The colonel wore several cardigans layered over his waistcoat, even though his parlor was warm. He presided very grandly over a tea table set with scones and small ham sandwiches. "My dear," he said happily, "we've saved up our butter ration for you."

They had. They had a whole little dish of butter along with jam for the scones. "Thank you," I said.

"Take plenty," he urged.

I took a tiny sliver.

"More than that," he ordered, as though he could see me.

I laughed. Stephen said, "She's got loads, don't worry," and after that it was easy to relax and eat.

Stephen said there was a new poster up by the train station. It showed Hitler listening to some British people's conversation. "'Careless talk costs lives,'" Stephen quoted. "That's what it says on the newsreels."

Susan had taken us to see the film *The Wizard of Oz,* but she'd let me stay in the lobby during the newsreel. I said, "Jamie worries about spies, but I don't know if they're really real. The government's so full of talk. How many spies do you think there are?"

"Hundreds!" the colonel said. "They're every-where! It was spies that sunk the *Royal Oak*! How else could a submarine have gotten into Scapa Flow?"

I knew that was what people said. "Yes, but—"

"You think we don't have spies right now in occupied France, in Germany itself? Of course we do! Stands to reason they'd have sent spies here."

I told him how I always looked out from the top of the hill, from where I could see such a long way.

He nodded. "You keep a lookout everywhere," he said. "I tell Stephen, pay attention to everything. You never know. One word in German, one false move—"

Stephen, grinning, helped me to another scone. I grinned back. Posters or newsreels or spies notwith-standing, it was hard to sit in a warm parlor with snow falling outside, and really believe in the war.

But by the end of January, German U-boats had sunk fifty-six ships in that month alone. Most were cargo ships trying to bring food and supplies to England.

In February, the Germans sunk another fifty-one. The shops looked sparse, coal supplies ran low, and the weather bore down on us like a cold heavy weight. We went to bed earlier and slept later in the mornings, just to avoid the black misery, until, finally, the days began to brighten.

Chapter 35

Maggie came home briefly at Easter. She was shocked by how much work I was doing, and also by the state the stables and house were in. Her house, not Susan's. "I've told Mum we've got to shut up most of the rooms," she said. I'd learned that Maggie was twelve years old. Top of her form in her current school, though she'd move to a different school for older girls next year. "Trying to keep on as we always have without enough staff is pointless. And Grimes must have help, or he'll drop over dead. It's not that you're not wonderful," she added, cutting off my protests, "but it's ridiculous; you'll drop dead too. She's still paying a gardener. He can help Grimes, and we'll turn the park into crops. We're supposed to be doing that anyhow."

I nodded. Susan had hired the vicar's gang of boys to dig up most of what was left of our back garden, and cut out the bushes in the front. We were planning a big Victory Garden, potatoes and turnips and carrots, Brussels sprouts and peas. Susan had already planted lettuce seeds on the dirt covering the roof of our shelter. Jamie was agitating for chickens, since eggs were getting scarce.

"Most of the evacuees in town are gone," Maggie added. "Mum said so. It makes her feel she hasn't done her job properly. Do you think you'll leave?"

I shook my head. "Our mum thinks we're safer here." I'd written to Maggie several times over the winter, but not once had I been able to tell her about Mam's disappearance. I didn't want Maggie to see me as rubbish, easy to throw away. "Friday's my birthday party," I added. "Will you come to tea? We're going to pretend I'm turning eleven."

Maggie already knew about my real birthday and my pretend birthday, but she still looked startled. "I thought you were eleven already," she said. "You seem older than ten, even though you're small."

This pleased me. "Really? Maybe you should tell Susan. Maybe we should pretend I'm twelve."

Maggie ignored this. "I'll be glad to come to the party. Home's dreadful, you can't imagine. I've never liked school, but now home's worse. Mum's in a funk all the time."

Every time I saw Lady Thorton she seemed in

constant motion, making lists, chivvying volunteers, commanding the WVS. When I said so, Maggie grimaced.

"Yes, that's her public face. In private she sort of slumps, and everything about her goes slow and dull. I didn't know she'd gotten like this. When she writes me letters they come from her public side."

Jonathan had finished his pilot's training, Maggie said. He had been sent to Stratford RAF base, which was north of London somewhere. "Mum can't get past it," she said. "Her brothers died in World War I. All three of them. Pilots."

I shuddered. "Maybe Jonathan should have gone into infantry."

"That's what Dad said, but Jonathan's like my uncles were, dead keen on flying. He always wanted to, even before the war. Mum told him she absolutely forbade it, but he signed up anyway. He was twenty-one, so she couldn't stop him.

"If he dies, Mum will die too," Maggie said. "She had two other boys after Jonathan, before me. All of them, all three, were named after my dead uncles, and then the other two died of typhoid when they were very small. Then came me, a girl, therefore useless. Mum's been afraid of this war since the day Jonathan was born."

"I'll keep an eye on her," I said. "I'll write you if your mam—your mum—gets worse. If I can tell she's worse."

Maggie nodded gratefully. "You don't know what it's like, being away from home and being so afraid." Then she gave me one of our long serious looks. "Or maybe you do."

"It's not really my birthday," I said, on the morning of my Celebration Tea.

"No," Susan agreed.

"I'm not really eleven yet. Or maybe I'm already eleven." If I thought about it, this made me angry, so I mostly didn't think about it.

"Those are the two choices," Susan agreed.

"I could be fourteen."

"Doubt it," Susan replied. "You'd probably have a bit of a bust if you were."

This made Jamie snort milk up his nose. I laughed too, and then I started to enjoy the day.

Susan had put a cloth on the kitchen table, and wildflowers Jamie picked in a vase in the center. She had saved up enough sugar from our rations to make a little cake. We had meat paste sandwiches, cut very thin, and fresh radishes, and tiny spoonfuls of custard sauce over the slices of cake. Susan made me a new dress from one that had been Becky's. Bright blue, like the springtime sky. She gave me a book called *The Wind in the Willows*. It was an old book, the cover faded and worn. When I opened it I saw her spidery handwriting on the flyleaf: *Susan Smith*. And then beneath that, in fresher ink, *To Ada with love. April 5, 1940.*

With love.

"It's one of my old books," Susan said, clearing her throat. "I'm sorry, I couldn't find a fresh copy in the shops."

I looked up. "I'd rather have this one," I said.

Maggie gave me a little carved wooden pony. "It's silly, it came from our nursery," she said, "but I saw it the other day, and I thought it looked like Butter."

It did look like Butter—Butter in summer, sleek and trotting through the grassy fields.

That night I put my new book on the shelf Susan had cleared for us in our bedroom. I put the pony on the windowsill so I could see him from the bed. I hung my dress in the wardrobe next to my other clothes.

I had so much. I felt so sad.

Early the next week, Hitler invaded Norway and Denmark. It felt like England had lost a battle, even though I'd never so much as heard of Norway or Denmark before. As spring continued, Germany took over Holland and Belgium as well. Winston Churchill became England's new prime minister. The war, which had begun to feel like memories of our flat in London, hazy and unreal, suddenly came into sharper focus. Susan had always listened to the news on the radio each evening but now Jamie and I paid close attention too. There still weren't bombs, in London or anywhere else, but the Germans were much nearer to England than they had been. Everyone thought we would be invaded next. The air force built pillboxes around our airfield, to defend it.

The government gave us seven rules:

1) Do not waste food.

2) Do not talk to strangers.

3) Keep all information to yourself.

4) Always listen to government instructions and carry them out.

5) Report anything suspicious to the police.

6) Do not spread rumors.

7) Lock away anything that might help the enemy if we are invaded.

"Like what?" Jamie asked. "Guns?"

"Yes, guns," Susan said. "Lady Thorton, for example—her husband has a whole roomful of guns for hunting game birds. She'll need to hide those away.

"We haven't got anything here the enemy would want," Susan continued. "We don't have anything dangerous or valuable.

"You aren't to worry," she said. "Even if the Germans do invade, they won't hurt children. They didn't hurt the children in Norway or Holland."

Somehow this didn't make us feel better at all.

The rumor in the village was that Holland had been full of German spies, sent in before the invasion to help it go smoothly. The spies were called "fifth columnists." I didn't know why. Fresh posters went up on the wall by the station, reminding us that England too might be full of spies. "Loose lips sink ships," the posters said.

Twenty-six ships had been sunk in March. Ten in April. It was fewer ships than earlier because now fewer ships were trying to get through the German blockade.

Jamie started wetting the bed again. Susan marched him over to the airfield to talk to some of the soldiers, thinking they would reassure him. Instead, the men told Jamie that of *course* there were spies in England. They told him that children were often better than adults at noticing things and that he, Jamie, needed to act like a soldier and keep a good lookout.

They told him to report back at once if he discovered anything unusual.

I didn't think Susan expected the RAF to turn Jamie into a snoop, but, anyway, he quit wetting the bed.

The government asked all the men who weren't already in the army to become Local Defence Volunteers. Stephen's colonel was angry that he couldn't join. "A man shouldn't be useless at a time like this," he fumed.

"It's not your fault you can't see," I told him. We'd run into them at the library. Susan was picking out more books for me, and Stephen was looking for things to read to the colonel.

"What difference does that make?" he said. "I still hate feeling helpless. And the boy tried to join up, and they wouldn't have him either."

I looked at Stephen in alarm. "How old are you?" I asked.

"Thirteen," he said. He dropped his voice to a whisper. "I didn't really try to join, I just told him I did. So he wouldn't be disappointed in me. It's nearly a full-time job taking care of him. Who does he think would queue for the groceries if I had to go off and drill?"

The Local Defence drilled with broomsticks

247

because they didn't have rifles. Stephen said the colonel had donated his guns from when he fought the Boer War. They were fifty years old and full of rust. "Useless," Stephen said. "But it made him feel better."

We had to queue for groceries every day now. Meat was on ration and a lot of other things were hard to find. Onions were so scarce they might as well have been solid gold. No one had realized that all England's onions were imported until they couldn't be imported anymore, and onions took a long time to grow from seed.

In the middle of May, Hitler invaded France. The British Army had over 370,000 soldiers stationed there. They fought, and the French fought, but the Germans pushed them back and back. Then came June, and Dunkirk. Later, people called it a miracle, but in our village it felt like a disaster.

Chapter 36

We woke to a vicious pounding on the door. Jamie clutched me. "Invasion?" he whispered.

My heart thumped in my ears. Should we hide? I was ready to push Jamie under the bed when I heard Lady Thorton yell from downstairs, "Susan! Get up, we need you! We need everyone!"

While Susan flung on her WVS uniform, I clambered down the stairs. Lady Thorton stood in the open doorway, breathing hard as though she'd been running even though her automobile was waiting in the drive. "What's happened?" I asked.

"A ship just docked in the village," Lady Thorton said. "Full of soldiers. From Dunkirk. And they were strafed on their way across the channel." She yelled up the stairs. "Susan!"

"Coming!" Susan hustled down, stuffing her hair beneath her WVS cap. She paused in the doorway and put her hand on my cheek. "You'll be okay?" she asked. "Both of you?"

"Yes," I said. I put my arm around Jamie and we watched Lady Thorton reverse her car in a whirl of dust. "It's not an invasion," I said.

Jamie looked up at me. "Strafed," he said.

Strafed meant shot at from above, by an airplane. I took a deep breath. "Yes," I said.

We'd listened with dread to the radio the night before. The British Army had retreated so far that it was now trapped against the ocean, near a French port called Dunkirk. The water was so shallow near the beach there that the Royal Navy, trying to rescue the soldiers, couldn't bring big ships close. The man on the radio had asked anyone with a small boat, one that could go close to shore, to loan it to the navy for getting the men away.

I'd seen our village's fishing boats. They could maybe carry a dozen men. I tried to imagine 370,000 men climbing onto boats a dozen at a time.

It couldn't happen. There would never be enough boats. If the Germans were strafing them, they would all die.

"I'll make breakfast," I said, putting on a cheerful face for Jamie's sake.

"I'm not hungry," he said.

"I'll make *sausages*." This brought a smile.

The sausages tasted odd. War sausages. Mostly oatmeal, I thought but didn't say. I wondered what sort of meat was actually in them.

We did the dishes and got dressed. We could hear planes taking off from the airfield, one after another. Dozens of planes. We went outside to watch them. They flew out toward the ocean and didn't come back.

"I want to go talk to the pilots," Jamie said.

"Not today," I told him. "They're busy."

He nodded. "They're strafing the Germans."

We stood watching the planes for a little while. I itched to be useful, like Susan. I knew I could do something.

Jamie looked at me piteously. "We can't just stay here," he said.

"No." Suddenly I knew what we could do. "You're going to go to Fred's," I said. "You'll help him in my place. I'm going to the village."

Jamie started to protest, but I cut him off. "I'm a junior WVS member," I said, making it up on the spot. "Lady Thorton expects me to do my duty, like a soldier. I expect you to do yours."

Jamie's eyes widened. He nodded.

"And you'll stay with Fred until Susan or I come for you," I said. "He's to feed you, and if we don't come tonight you're to sleep there. Tell him I said so."

Jamie nodded. "Can I take Butter?"

"Of course." He rode Butter around the field often enough. I helped him saddle and bridle the pony.

After that I put on my sky-blue dress. I plaited my own hair. I stuffed a pillowcase full of the cloth scraps Susan was supposed to be sewing into bandages, and I took my crutches and set off for town.

I saw the newsreels later. They didn't upset me, not when I'd already helped Dunkirk soldiers first-hand. But those newsreels showed a lie. In them, the soldiers evacuating Dunkirk looked tired, but happy. Under their tin hats their faces were dirty, but their eyes shone bright. They grinned and waved and gave thumbs-ups to the camera. Stalwart British fighters, heroic and grateful to be home.

Maybe there were soldiers like that somewhere. The ones in our village were shot, dead or dying; others were sick from the long terrible retreat, the days without food or water.

The men on that first ship who could walk had carried their severely injured comrades into the town hall, the place where I'd stood on evacuation day, waiting for someone to choose me.

When I got to town I saw a woman in a WVS uniform go inside the hall. I followed, pushing open the door.

I gagged. The smell of blood hung across the room like a heavy iron fog, but worse than that—people don't tell you, they don't write about it and they don't put it in the newsreels—when men are horribly injured, they lose control of their bowels. They mess themselves the way babies do. The stench made my eyes water and my stomach churn.

The whole room was filled with wounded men on stretchers. I saw Dr. Graham working among army medics and the WVS. I saw Lady Thorton, her face streaked with blood. I saw Susan, who looked up and saw me. "Get out of here," she barked.

Already I could see what some of the women were doing—peeling away the soldiers' pants and cleaning their naked backsides. They wouldn't want me helping with that. I nodded to Susan and slipped back outside.

The street was full of less-injured men. Townspeople directed them into the pub, the library, any building with open space. Men stumbled, collapsed, cried. "Miss," said one, looking up at me. He sat on the curb with a blood-soaked leg held stiff in front of him. "Water?"

I went into the pub. It was full of soldiers and people from the village. If anyone noticed me, they didn't care. I tossed my crutches and pillowcase behind the bar, found a pitcher and filled it, grabbed a mug, limped to the street, and gave the water to the soldier. He drank until the pitcher was empty.

I went back and forth, carrying water. Eventually the publican's daughter, who seemed about my age, came out with a heavy bucket. "You stand here with the mug," she said. "I'll bring buckets back and forth."

Soldiers clustered around me, reeking, stinking, filthy, their uniforms crusted with sweat and blood. They drank and drank. Cracked lips, haunted eyes. Another bucket of water, and another. The publican's daughter brought more mugs, which I dipped into the buckets and passed around. When the flow of men who could still walk ceased—I later learned that if they could, they went on to the train station, and then to an army base north of us—I went into the pub, and tried to help the soldiers there. It was the same with them as in the hall: blood, filth, exhaustion. Daisy—that was the publican's daughter's name—and I went down the rows giving out drinks, water first and eventually tea. Back and forth, back and forth down the rows.

It seemed impossible that all these men could come

from one ship, even if it had been a big ship. When I said so to Daisy, another villager cut in, "We're on the third or fourth ship by now. They're unloading wherever they can dock, and going back for more."

Sometime after dark Daisy's mother insisted we rest in the kitchen. She sat us at a long table and pushed plates of food in front of us. "Eat," she commanded.

Daisy sat unmoving. I was trying to will myself to pick up a fork when I saw something splash onto Daisy's plate. I looked up. Tears streamed down Daisy's face.

"None of that," Daisy's mother said. "Won't help any."

"But they're dying," Daisy said.

"No, they're not. They look awful, but men can look much worse and still live. You'd be surprised. Eat and rest, or I'll send you both to bed."

We ate. "You've ruined your dress," Daisy said.

I looked down. My sky-blue dress was covered with dark smudges and smears of grime. "It's my favorite," I said.

Daisy nodded. "It's pretty."

When we'd rested we went back out and made another round of tea.

One soldier looked up at me, his eyes very bright. "Miss?" he said. "Could you do me a favor, and write a letter for me? My hands feel a little numb."

"Daisy will," I said. My handwriting was still so slow and clumsy. I went to fetch Daisy, and some paper and a pen. We came back and the man's eyes were closed.

He was *dead*.

He died, right there on the floor of the pub. He didn't even look wounded—he wasn't bleeding. One of the other soldiers undid his tunic, searching for a heartbeat, and there wasn't any blood at all. But he was dead. The soldiers found a blanket and pulled it over his head.

I couldn't breathe. Dead, when he'd just been talking to me. Dead, when he'd wanted to write a letter. A wave of grief washed over me. I started to go away in my head, to somewhere safe, to Butter or Jamie or wherever, but Daisy grabbed my hand and squeezed it hard, and I came back.

"It's really a war now," Daisy whispered. I nodded. One of the soldiers called for tea. Daisy and I brought it to him.

Most of the ships that docked at our village the week of the Dunkirk evacuations weren't as bad off as the first few, but all of them contained at least some badly injured men. The ships arrived at all hours. We went from crisis to crisis; the hall never emptied. The Spitfires from our airfield took off and landed in waves, constantly, day and night, flying out to protect the troopships as much as possible. Meanwhile the entire village fed and tended the soldiers.

Before midnight on that first day, Susan found me at the pub. Daisy's mother told her what we'd been doing. Reluctantly, Susan allowed me to stay in the village. Daisy's mother said I could sleep at the pub, with them; the WVS was sleeping in shifts in their headquarters down the street.

"You're a little girl," Susan said. "You shouldn't have to see all this."

"I'm old enough. I'm helping." I wanted to tell her about the dead soldier, but I was afraid she'd make me leave.

She gave me a long look. "Yes," she said. "You are."

The next morning Susan used the pub's telephone to call Lady Thorton's house and speak to Fred and Jamie. And then we carried on. Whenever Daisy or I grew too exhausted to continue, we crept back to the kitchen and slept on the bench by the door. When we woke, we went back to work. Everyone did. It was lucky Jamie was safe with Fred. Lucky we'd put Bovril outside, where he could hunt. Susan and I stayed with the soldiers. It was our turn to fight the war.

In the end, 330,000 British soldiers were saved.

Winston Churchill called it England's "finest hour." It was hard, listening to him on the radio, safely home with Jamie once again, to think that there had been anything fine about the shiploads of desperate and dying men. But at the same time, I felt different. There was a Before Dunkirk version of me and an After Dunkirk version. The After Dunkirk version was stronger, less afraid. It had been awful, but I hadn't quit. I had persisted. In battle I had won.

Chapter 37

Several days later, when Susan and I went into the village, I stopped at the pub to say hello to Daisy. "Oh, dearie," said her mother, pulling me against her large bosom and kissing the top of my head. "I've sent her away," she said. To Susan she added, "You'd better send yours too."

The village was evacuating its own children.

Across the channel, Hitler's army waited, less than thirty miles away. He invaded the Channel Islands, Guernsey and Jersey, which belonged to England.

The Channel Islands surrendered.

Kent, which was the part of England where we were, was the closest bit to the German Army in France. When Hitler invaded, he would land in Kent.

Susan said nothing to Daisy's mother, but later told Jamie and me not to worry. If our mother wanted us to go somewhere else, that was one thing, but until Susan heard from our mother, we were staying put.

A few days later Lady Thorton came to try to make Jamie and me go. All the other evacuees and nearly all the village children were leaving. The WVS, Lady Thorton said, would find a home for us somewhere safe.

"Their mother won't know where they are," Susan protested.

"Of course she will," Lady Thorton said. "I'll see that you get their new address, and whenever she contacts you, you can pass it on."

Susan hesitated. "I'm not sure."

Lady Thorton's nose narrowed the way it did when she was angry. "There *will* be an invasion," she said, in a tightly clipped tone. "German soldiers in our streets, in our homes. War in our streets, quite possibly. The children should be as far away as we can send them. Margaret isn't coming home this summer. She's going straight to her new school."

I felt a pang of regret. I'd been expecting to see Maggie soon.

Lady Thorton said, "You must send them away."

Beneath the regret came a bigger wave of emotion, coiling up, rising in my gut. I didn't know what it was. I didn't know what it meant. I looked out the window and frantically tried to think of Butter.

". . . things worse than bombs," Susan was saying.

Lady Thorton shook her head. "War is no time for sentiment."

"Is it sentiment?" Susan asked. Her voice sounded far away behind the humming in my ears. Susan put a hand on my shoulder. "Look at them," Susan said. "Look at Ada. If she gets put with the wrong person she'll go right back to where she was."

I shook my head, struggling to stay with them, to hear them above my increasing panic. But Lady Thorton didn't reply. When I risked a glance at her she was staring at Susan with an expression I couldn't read.

"She isn't easy," Susan said, "but I'll fight for her. I do fight for her. Someone has to."

At last Lady Thorton spoke. "I see," she said quietly. "I'm not sure you're correct, but I see what you're saying. But the boy—"

"No," Susan said. "Separating them would kill them both."

When Lady Thorton had left, Susan sat Jamie and me down beside her on the sofa. She said, "Listen. I am not sending you away."

She talked a long time after that. I heard nothing beyond the words "not sending you away."

The wave inside me flattened out. I could breathe again.

"How do you feel about it?" Susan asked me.

How did I feel? I had no idea. I didn't know the words to explain. *I was choking and now I can breathe.* Susan waited for me to say something. I still felt dizzy, overwhelmed. I swallowed. "I guess I'd rather stay here," I said.

"Good," Susan said, "because I'm not giving you a choice."

Susan had been right that all the green leaves and grass came back in summertime. The weather was glorious. Butter's pasture reached his knees, and the vegetables in our Victory Garden thrived.

Fred found an old bicycle in one of the sheds at Thorton House and fixed it up for Jamie to ride. School had closed for good, since most of the children were gone, so Jamie came with me every day to help Fred. The former gardener had proved useless around horses, frightened of them and therefore inclined to smack them around. He'd been called up anyhow; Fred was alone again. Lady Thorton had sold two horses, and put down three more who were past being ridden, but that still left a lot of work to do. The best pastures had been taken over for crops. The government sent Land Girls to take the place of the enlisted male farm workers. They moved into the old stable boys' apartments, but they only helped with the farming on the estate, not the horses. "Horses aren't important these days," said Fred.

Jamie was finally permanently and completely banned from the airfield. They were too busy to have him around. Planes took off in bunches all day and all night. We could see them high in the sky, tiny specks patrolling the channel. Watching, waiting, for the invasion that would come.

I struggled to fall asleep in the long, bright summer nights. Jamie and Bovril snored in unison, loudly. One night, when the noise grew too much to bear, I crept downstairs to the slightly darker living room. Susan sat on the sofa, her legs curled beneath her, staring into nothing. It was not the deep sad staring from the year before. "Can't sleep?" she asked when she saw me.

I shook my head. Susan patted the sofa beside her. I walked across the room and stood in front of her, my good foot and the crutch tips deep in the plush rug, the toes of my bad foot barely brushing the ground.

"Everyone still thinks I should send you away," Susan said.

I nodded. Lady Thorton said so often. I went to Susan's WVS meetings sometimes, to help sew, and

Lady Thorton made a noise in the back of her throat every time she saw me.

"Part of me does agree," Susan continued. "I know they mean well. But I also understand now why some of the mothers from London took their evacuated children back so soon. Some things you've got to face as a family."

Hitler was in Paris. He could be in London next week.

"For the longest time," Susan went on, "I thought I was neglecting you. I didn't take care of you the way my mother took care of my brothers and me. My mother watched me all the time. She always kept me neatly dressed. She ironed my *shoelaces*. She would never have let you run wild the way I have.

"But now, when I look at you, I think I didn't do so badly. I think you wouldn't have liked being raised the way my mother raised me. What do you think, Ada?"

I sat down on the sofa. "I never know," I said. "When I'm not thinking, everything's clear in my head, but as soon as I try to look at it I get confused." I leaned against the back of the sofa.

"I understand," Susan said. "Sometimes I feel like that too."

I leaned my head against her, the tiniest bit. She

didn't move. I leaned a little bit more. She put her arm around my shoulders, so that I was nestled against her. As I drifted into sleep I thought I felt her lips brush the top of my head.

The first air raid was worse than Christmas Eve.

Chapter 38

It came the second week of July. It had been a hot day, so we had kept the windows wide open and the blackout down. For once I'd fallen into a sound, dreamless sleep.

Whoop-WHOOP! Whoop—WHOOP! Whoop-WHOOP! The sirens at the airfield wailed, louder and louder. You'd have thought one was in our bedroom. Jamie jumped up, scrambling to keep hold of Bovril, who thrashed and scratched in an effort to get free. I grabbed my crutches. Susan came flying in, her dressing gown flapping. "Hurry, hurry," she said.

I couldn't hurry. Going downstairs took time. My hands shook. I wouldn't be fast enough. I would be bombed.

Jamie ran ahead, but Susan waited for me. "It's all right," she said. "Don't panic."

Across the living room, out the back door. Jamie ducked into the Anderson shelter and stuffed Bovril into his basket. The cat howled. He sounded like a baby screaming in pain.

I stood at the door of the shelter. I'd never yet gone inside. I hated it, it scared me, it was so much like the cabinet under the sink at home. The one with the roaches. I could never see them or stop them.

"Ada," Susan said, behind me, "MOVE."

I couldn't do it. I couldn't go inside. Not into that damp shelter, that smelled exactly like the cabinet. Not into that darkness. Not into that pain.

The siren wailed. Jamie shouted, "Ada, hurry!"

A noise like the plane exploding. Bombs. Real bombs, here in Kent, German bombs everyone feared. Here in the cabinet under the sink—

Susan picked me up and carried me down the stairs. The smell enveloped me. I could feel the cramped cabinet, the roaches. I could hear Mam laughing while I screamed.

I screamed. Another bomb. More screams. From Jamie? From me? How would I know? The memory of the cabinet seemed real, seemed to be happening right at that moment. I could *see* the cabinet, feel myself being shoved inside. Terror enveloped my brain.

Suddenly I felt something tight around me. A blanket, a rough wool blanket. Susan wrapped me in it the way she had on Christmas Eve, tight, round and round. "Shh," she said. "Shh." She put her arms around me and laid me on a bench and then half sat on me, squishing me between her backside and the shelter wall. "We're all here, we're safe," she said. She took Jamie onto her lap. "It's okay, Jamie, she's just frightened. It's okay." Jamie whimpered. "We're safe," Susan said. "It's okay."

The pressure of the blanket soothed me. Gradually I came back to the shelter, to Jamie and Susan. I stopped screaming. My heart didn't pound so hard. I breathed the smell of the wool blanket, wet from my tears, instead of the shelter-cabinet dampness.

From outside we heard another blast, farther away, and the *ack-ack* from the antiaircraft guns at the airfield.

"We're okay," Susan said wearily. "We're okay."

When the all-clear sounded two hours later, Susan and I were still wide-awake. Jamie had fallen asleep on Susan's lap. She carried him back to the house. I walked beside her, trailing the blanket like a cape. We lay down in the living room, too worn out to climb the stairs.

Late the next morning, when we woke, Susan said, "Ada, there will be more bombs. We will have to go into the shelter. You'd better get used to it."

I shuddered. I couldn't imagine doing that again.

"What set you off?" Susan asked.

"Mam's cabinet—the way it smells—" I made myself go somewhere else in my head, fast, before panic overwhelmed me. Butter. I imagined riding Butter.

Susan tapped my chin. "We can change the smell."

She went to the market and bought aromatic herbs, rosemary, lavender, and sage. She hung them in the shelter, upside down from the edges of the benches, and their smell filled the little room even after they were crumbly and dry. I couldn't smell the dampness anymore. It helped. I still panicked. Susan still always wrapped me in a blanket. But usually I could keep from screaming, and I didn't actually see the cabinet in my head. It was still awful, but I didn't frighten Jamie.

That was important, because we went into the shelter nearly every night from that first time. The Battle of Britain had begun.

Hitler had figured out he couldn't land his invading army until he'd conquered the Royal Air Force. Otherwise, our planes would bomb his ships and troops while they were landing. Once he'd gotten rid of our planes, invading England would be easy. The Germans had a lot more airplanes and pilots than the British did. They had different kinds of planes, though, and their fighter planes had shorter ranges than ours. This meant that they could only reach the southeastern corner of England before they had to turn back for more fuel. They could only shoot our planes and bomb our airfields in Kent.

The airfields were their main targets. Every plane they destroyed, whether in the air or parked on the ground, brought them one step closer to invasion; every runway they destroyed gave our pilots one less place to safely land. Our airfield was hit that very first day; the bombs ripped through two storage sheds and left craters the size of small tanks in the grass runways. Fortunately all the air crews found shelter. Once the all-clear sounded, the crews worked through the night, shoveling debris into the blast holes. By morning planes could safely land again.

It was July, and the world was green and lovely. I rode Butter through fields of waving grass, up our hill to where I could see the blue sea glittering in the bright sunlight. Wild roses grew in the hedgerows, and the air felt heavy with their scent. The breeze blew and I could feel perfectly happy, except that now I always watched for planes as well as spies. They hadn't come in daytime yet, but I knew they could.

Susan didn't like me riding out, but she didn't want to forbid it either. Our home was so close to the airfield, I figured I was safer farther away. When I said so, she looked grim. "I should send you away," she said.

It was hard enough to cope with Susan. How would I ever cope without her?

What if we got sent back home?

I stared at the tips of my shoes. "I can't leave Butter," I said.

Susan sighed. "You survived without a pony in London."

I lifted my gaze to look at her. I had survived. Maybe. Could I do it again? Back in that one room, I hadn't known all I was missing.

"I know," Susan said softly. "It's why I'm keeping you here."

"There's things worse than bombs," I said, remembering what I'd heard her say before.

"I think so," Susan said. "And Kent's a big place, they can't bomb every inch of it." But she looked out the window toward the airfield, and her eyes creased with worry.

Chapter 39

Nights in the shelter, night after night. It was impossible to sleep through the explosions and the gunfire. Susan had a flashlight, but flashlights needed batteries, and batteries were hard to find. Instead she lit a candle inside a flowerpot, and by its dim light read to us. *Peter Pan. A Secret Garden. The Wind in the Willows.* Some were books she got from the library; others came from her own bookshelves. On his own, Jamie was reading *Swiss Family Robinson* over again. "We're like them," he said one night, as the candlelit flickered off the shelter's tin walls. "We're in our cave, safe and warm."

I shuddered. I had wrapped myself in a sheet, because it was too hot for a blanket. I felt warm, but not safe. I never felt safe in the shelter. "You are, though," Susan said. "You feel safer in your bedroom, but you're actually much safer in the shelter."

It didn't matter how I felt. She made me go into the shelter every time the sirens wailed.

Men came and removed all the signposts from the roads around the village, so that when Hitler invaded he wouldn't know where he was.

When he invaded, we were to bury our radio. Jamie had already dug a hole for it in the garden. When Hitler invaded we were to say nothing, do nothing to help the enemy.

If he invaded while I was out riding, I was to return home at once, as fast as possible by the shortest route. I'd know it was an invasion, not an air raid, because all the church bells would ring.

"What if the Germans take Butter?" I asked Susan.

"They won't," she said, but I was sure she was lying.

"Bloody huns," Fred muttered, when I went to help with chores. "They come here, I'll stab 'em with a pitchfork, I will." Fred was not happy. The riding horses, the Thortons' fine hunters, were all out to grass, and the grass was good, but the hayfields had been turned over to wheat and Fred didn't know how he'd feed the horses through the winter. Plus the Land Girls staying in the loft annoyed him. "Work twelve hours a day, then go out dancing," he said. "Bunch of lightfoots. In my day girls didn't act like that."

I thought the Land Girls seemed friendly, but I knew better than to say so to Fred.

You could get used to anything. After a few weeks, I didn't panic when I went into the shelter. I quit worrying about the invasion. I put Jamie up behind me on Butter and we searched the fields for shrapnel or bullets or bombs. Once we came across an airplane shot down in a hops field. Soldiers had already surrounded it by the time we got there, and were keeping civilians away. "A Messerschmidt," Jamie said, eyes gleaming. "Wonder where the pilot went." The pilot had bailed out; the plane's canopy was open.

"Caught him," one of the soldiers said, overhearing. "Prisoner of war. No troubles."

On a day in early August Susan went to a WVS meeting. Jamie was tending the garden—he loved it—and I took off on Butter for my daily ride.

I went to the top of the hill. I paused, the way I always did, to search the sea and sky. No airplanes. No big boats. But then I saw something in the distance, something small on the surface of the ocean. A tiny boat, a rowboat, pulling for shore. I watched it, wondering. It was headed not for the town harbor, but for one of the barbed-wire sections of the beach. Was the person lost? Surely he knew better than to land where there were could be mines. I kept watching, frowning. The man—it looked like a man, I thought—in the boat continued to row straight for shore. Surely he could see the village from the water. Surely he knew it would be safer there.

Unless, I thought, my blood running cold, he was a spy.

A spy! I couldn't believe it. I didn't believe it. I always looked for spies from the hill. It was a habit. But that didn't mean, despite the posters, despite the rumors, that I actually expected to ever see a spy. But yet—a single rowboat, so far out—where had he come from? Did he get dropped off by a submarine—a German submarine? If he wasn't a spy, why was he headed toward the deserted beach?

I heard Susan's voice in my head. "Improbable," it said. That mean not likely.

Still, it was one of the rules: Report anything suspicious at once. I turned Butter down the face of the hill, weaving through brush and tall grass, trying to keep the little boat in sight. It disappeared from my view as I got lower, and I sped up, cantering along the road that led to the barricaded beach. I stopped Butter in a copse of trees just as the beach came into view.

It was low tide, and the sand stretched out wide and flat for a mile along the shoreline. Right in the center of the sand, the man stepped from his rowboat. He carried a suitcase and had a rucksack on his back. As I watched, he shoved the rowboat back into the water. The sea was quiet. The boat floated high above the gentle waves, and began to drift sideways, following the shore.

I swallowed hard.

The man—an ordinary-looking man, at least from the distance—took something from his rucksack. He unfolded it and used whatever it was to dig a hole in the beach. He put the suitcase into the hole. Covered the hole with sand. Walked cautiously up the sand dunes toward the barbed wire. I couldn't see what happened next, but suddenly the man was on the other side of the fence, walking down the road toward me.

I turned Butter and galloped away.

I could have gone to the airfield, but the police station was closer and I knew where it was: near the school, near the shop where I'd had tea. I kept Butter to a canter even over the cobblestoned main street. I pulled him to a halt at the station, wrapped his reins around the handrail, and hurried up the steps as best as I could. I didn't have my crutches. "I think I found a spy!" I said to the first person I saw, a portly man seated behind a large wooden desk. "A spy on the beach!"

The portly man turned toward me. "Get ahold of yourself, miss!" he said. "I can't understand you the way you're gabbling."

I grabbed the edge of his desk for balance. I repeated my words.

The man looked me up and down. Particularly down, at my bad foot in its odd homemade shoe. I fought the urge to hide it.

"How was it you saw this spy?" he asked. He had a little smile on his face. I realized he did not believe me.

"I was out on my pony—" I began. I told the whole story, the hill where I always kept a lookout, the little boat, the suitcase buried in the sand.

"On your pony," the man said, nodding, his smile widening into a smirk. "Watch a lot of newsreels, do you? Listen to the scary stories on the radio?"

He thought I was lying, or, at best, exaggerating. And now he was staring at my bad foot again. I felt a wave of heat climb up my neck.

I thought of what Susan would do. I drew myself up, taller, and glared at the man, and I said, "My bad foot's a long way from my brain."

The man blinked.

I said, "I would like to speak to your commanding officer. The government asks us to report anything suspicious, and that's what I am going to do. If you won't listen, I want to talk to someone who will."

The second police officer took me more seriously. "We'll go in the squad car," he said. "See if we can find him." He asked if I needed help getting to the car.

"No, thank you," I said. I walked as straight as I could manage, even though it hurt like crazy. The officer put me in the front seat beside him and together we started down the road. We'd hardly gotten out of town when we came across the man I'd seen, walking down the road with perfect ease. I pointed him out to the officer.

"You're sure?" the officer asked.

For a moment I wasn't. I hadn't really gotten a close look at the man's face. But he felt like the right person. I nodded. The officer stopped his car and got out. "Papers, please," he said.

"Really?" said the man, in perfect English with the accent Lady Thorton used. "Why ever for?"

"Routine," the officer said.

The man raised his eyebrow as if it were all a joke,

but reached into his pocket readily enough. He pulled his identity card out of a battered leather wallet. "I'm just on a bit of a walking holiday," he said, indicating the rucksack on his back. "My ration card's in there if you want me to fish it out."

He could not sound more English. He could not look more English. And yet—

"Sir," I said to the officer. He came over to the window on the passenger side, and leaned in.

"I'm sorry, miss," he said, shaking his head, "but I think you've—"

I said, "His trouser cuffs are wet. And they're full of sand."

No one went on the beaches anymore. No one ever. It wasn't allowed.

The officer's smile disappeared. For a moment I thought he was angry with me, but I was wrong. The next thing I knew the man from the beach was handcuffed and bundled into the back of the car. He protested vehemently in his perfect English voice.

Back at the station, patient Butter still stood tied to the porch rail. The officer told me to go on home. "We'll handle it from here, miss."

I wanted to tell Susan, but I wasn't sure how. I put it off so that I could think about it more. We were halfway through dinner that evening when the police knocked on the door.

It was my second officer, and another. "We need to speak with your daughter, ma'am."

I got up quickly. Susan looked stunned. Jamie looked delighted.

"We need you to help us locate the buried parcel," my officer said. So I went again in a squad car, this time all the way to the beach. I showed them where I'd stood with Butter, watching, and I tried to show them where I thought the man had landed with his boat. The tide was high now and everything looked different.

"We'll have to get the army to dig it up anyhow," the other officer said. "For all we know, the beach is mined." He drove along the edge of the barbed-wire fence. We got out near where I thought the man had gone through, and walked up and down the road until we found a footprint. The officer marked it with a piece of cloth tied to the fence, and then took me home.

I paused before I got out of the car. "Will you let me know what happens to the man?"

The officers shook their heads. "It'll be a secret, miss."

"Will you let me know if he really is a spy?"

They looked at each other, and nodded. "But you're to stay quiet about it," one said.

I nodded. "Loose Lips Sink Ships," I said. I went in to make my explanations to Susan.

She was waiting for me on the purple sofa. She listened to the whole story. Then she put her hands on either side of my face. She smiled at me, and she said, "Oh, Ada. I am so proud."

The very next afternoon, someone knocked on our door again. It was a police officer—not the one who had helped me, but the fat one who'd sat at his desk and thought I was making things up. "I need to apologize to your daughter, ma'am," he said. When he saw me, he swept off his hat and bowed. "I should have believed you," he said. "I'm sorry. A grateful nation thanks you for your service."

With great ceremony, he handed me an onion.

Chapter 40

The army had found the suitcase buried in the sand. It contained a radio transmitter, the sort spies used to send coded messages across the channel. The perfect Englishman really *had* been a spy.

I became a hero. The RAF men at the airfield brought me chocolate; the WVS women pooled together a tablespoon of sugar each, and gave me a whole bag. Daisy's mother from the pub hugged me whenever she saw me, and every time I went into the village I was greeted with smiles and shouts of, "There's our little spy-catcher!" or "There's our good lass!"

It was as if I'd been born in the village. As if I'd been born with two strong feet. As if I really was someone important, someone loved.

Jamie made me repeat the story over and over again. "Tell me," he'd beg. "Tell me your hero story."

Maggie wrote from her school. *Ooh, I wish I'd been*

with you! I might have been, you know, if I'd been home.

I wish you had been, I wrote back.

You wouldn't mind sharing the honors? she replied.

I wouldn't have minded at all. It would have been easier. *Hero* wasn't a word I was used to hearing. The admiration was interesting, but the attention made me feel unsettled.

"Say it again," Jamie said, giggling. "Tell me what you told the first officer."

"He looked at my bad foot," I said, "and I said, 'my foot's a long way from my brain.'"

"And you were right," Jamie said.

"Yes," said Susan. "She was."

Of course, the part that was frightening was that there had been an actual spy. A real spy. Sent to make the invasion easier. When the air raid sirens started up again it was hard not to be very afraid.

"But you caught him," Jamie said.

"I caught one spy," I said. *"One."* The sirens had started earlier than usual that evening, while we were still eating; we'd carried our plates to the shelter with us.

"An' now he's dead," Jamie said, chewing with his mouth open. "We took him out to a field, lined him up, and pow!" He mimed firing a gun. I flinched.

"Probably not," Susan said. "I asked."

Jamie narrowed his eyes. "What'd we do, then?"

"Nobody will say for sure."

I picked through the boiled potatoes on my plate. Susan had left the peels on, because peeling potatoes wasted food and we weren't allowed to waste food in wartime. I didn't like the peels. England had a lot of potatoes; we were supposed to eat them every day.

"Probably turned him," Susan said. "Made him a double agent. That means the government would force him to send false messages back to Germany, with that transmitter of his."

"They'd make him tell lies," I said.

"Yes," Susan said.

Jamie scowled. "I wouldn't do that. If the Germans caught me—"

"I would," I said. "If he doesn't lie, they'll shoot him. I'd lie if I had to."

Now sometimes the German planes attacked in daylight. If they were far away Jamie and I stood in the field and watched them, shielding our eyes against the sun. The planes looked like swarms of insects buzzing in circles in the sky, until one plummeted, leaving a trail of smoke. From such a distance I couldn't tell the English planes from the German ones, but Jamie could.

"One of ours," he'd say, or, "One of theirs."

Sometimes we could see the puff of a parachute opening, as a pilot bailed out. I always hoped for that puff, even when the plane was German.

Two of the pilots who had come for Christmas dinner had died. When Jamie found out, he cried himself to sleep. I thought of their faces, how they'd laughed and played with Jamie. Unlike Jamie, I hadn't remembered their names. I'd been too upset, that day, about my green dress.

I understood why I'd been upset on Christmas. I'd felt overwhelmed; I really couldn't help myself. But now, thinking back, it seemed a little silly to be unhappy about a dress when the pilots were dead. If I had it to do over, I would at least have learned their names.

England lost planes every day. Germany lost more. New planes flew into our airfield from the north of England. New pilots came straight from their training fields. They went up every day, and not all of them came back.

We had to win this battle, Susan said, or we would

lose the war. On the radio Prime Minister Churchill said, "Never in the field of human conflict was so much owed by so many to so few." It meant the pilots were saving us all. It meant they were the only thing keeping the Germans away.

September came. I quit attracting so much attention in the village. A week ago British planes had attacked Berlin: The first time we'd taken the war onto German soil. Fred cackled in delight. "We'll show 'em now." A small piece of a damaged German plane had come down on the edge of one of Thorton's wheat fields. Fred gave it to me to take to Jamie.

"How do you know it's German?" I asked, turning the scrap of metal over in my hands.

"I saw the bugger," Fred said. "He was heading back over the channel, trailing parts of his airplane as he went."

It was bad training to let Butter run when he was close to home, but that day I did it. I felt so happy. The sun was warm, I couldn't see planes or hear sirens, and Jamie would be so pleased to have the chunk of German plane. Butter galloped happily, his ears pricked. I'd been practicing my jumping all summer, and even though Fred hadn't given me permission yet, I knew we were ready. Instead of slowing Butter for the pasture gate I turned him toward the stone wall, and urged him forward.

He flew it. We'd jumped the wall at last.

Across the field I could see Susan standing in the back garden with Jamie and an adult I didn't know. I kicked Butter on, flying down the field. "Jamie!" I yelled. "I brought you a piece of a Messerschmidt!" I pulled Butter up and patted his neck, laughing. "Did you see us jump?" I asked Susan. "Did you?"

Then I recognized the woman standing beside her.

Mam.

Chapter 41

Mam.

I didn't know what to think. I steadied Butter in front of the garden wall, my hands on the reins, and looked at her. She looked back at me, shading her eyes with her hand. Her expression, of mingled anger and disinterest, didn't change. "Hello," I said.

She scowled. "Who're you?"

She didn't recognize me.

I dismounted Butter, landing carefully on my good left foot. I untied my crutches from the back of the saddle and swung myself forward, over the garden wall. "I'm Ada," I said.

Her expression turned to outrage as she realized who I was.

"What the 'ell's this?" she said. "Just who do you think you are?"

Jamie was holding Mam's hand. Jamie looked so hopeful.

"Coming in on a pony!" Mam said. "Like little Princess Margaret, are you now?"

"I learned to ride," I said. "I go sidesaddle so it doesn't hurt my—"

Mam thrust a battered envelope under my nose. "And this," she said. "What's the meaning of this, eh?"

I looked. It was one of Susan's letters. It was her handwriting on the envelope.

"Want some kind of operation, do you?" Mam said.

My heart leaped. "They can fix my foot. The doctor said—"

"Like 'ell they can," Mam said. "Isn't nothing going to fix that foot. First I get a letter says now I have to pay the government for taking my kids away, nineteen shillings a week and the government wants me to pay—"

"No one will make you—" Susan interjected.

"—and then here's this. Sent to the wrong place, just got it, I did, and what is it but someone with the bloody cheek to be tellin' me what to do with my kids. And then here you are, all dressed up, sittin' on a pony, nose in the air, actin' for all the world like you're better than everybody—"

"No, Mam," I said.

"—like you're better than *me*."

"No, Mam."

"Come on," Mam said. "We're goin' home."

Susan tried to argue. Mam turned on her and glared. "You're tellin' me where I can take my own kids? You? A lazy slut in a fancy house—" Mam went on from there, telling Susan off every possible way.

I felt myself grow cold, distant, far from all of them. My mind folded in on itself. But no, I had to stay present, I hadn't taken care of Butter. I started back to the pasture. "Where do you think you're goin'?" Mam said.

"I need to untack Butter. He can't stay with his saddle on."

"Like 'ell! Come back here, we're catching the next train."

I still moved toward Butter. Mam walloped me, caught me straight between the shoulders with a hard blow. I hadn't expected it, and I flew forward, scattering my crutches and scuffing my palms in the dirt. Jamie cried out. Tears came to my eyes. I'd forgotten what being hit was like. I staggered to my feet.

"I'll take care of Butter," Susan said.

"C'mon, Ada," Mam said. She had her hand on Jamie's neck, so I couldn't see his face. She marched him toward the side gate.

"Wait!" Susan said, turning back. "They need their things."

"They don't need nothing," Mam replied. "Dressed up like toffs. You've done them no favors, lettin' them get above themselves. They don't need no things, not where they're goin'."

Susan ran into the house anyway. She came out carrying her copy of *Swiss Family Robinson*. "Take this," she said to Jamie, thrusting it at him. "It's yours."

Mam eyed the book suspiciously. "He don't want that," she said. "What would he do with that?"

"I don't want it," Jamie echoed. His hopeful expression had vanished; he looked petrified. "I don't!"

"No," I said. "He doesn't." *Don't make him take it,* I silently begged Susan. *It'll be worse for him if you do.*

Susan looked at me. Her face went blank. She slipped the book under her arm. "I'll keep it for you, Jamie," she said. "Ada, I'll take care of Butter. I promise. I won't let his feet grow long again."

Mam pushed Jamie through the gate.

Susan said, "No."

She said, "You don't have to go. Ada. Jamie. You can stay with me. I'll fix it. I promise. You can stay."

Mam scowled. "Think you can steal my kids, do you?"

"I'll go to the police," Susan said. "They'll listen to you, Ada. They'll listen to us. You can stay."

The pause that followed this seemed to last a lifetime. Mam sucked in her breath. Jamie snuffled. I
looked at Susan and I said, "You didn't want us."

Susan looked straight back at me. She said, "That
was last year. I want you now."

But Jamie was holding Mam's hand. The police
might let me stay with Susan, but they'd have no
reason to take Jamie from Mam. Mam never locked
Jamie up.

I said, "I can't leave Jamie."

Susan looked back at me and very slowly nodded.
Mam muttered something under her breath. She
yanked Jamie down the road. I followed. When I
looked back Susan was already on the other side of
the garden wall, unbuckling the girth of my saddle.
She didn't look up. She didn't say good-bye.

Chapter 42

When we got to the end of the drive Mam stopped. "What're those?" she said, pointing to my crutches.

"I walk faster with them," I said.

She snorted. "Like you need to walk."

I said, "I *can* walk."

"Not for long, missy," Mam said. "Not for long."

The train to London was even slower and more crowded than the one we'd been evacuated on. Servicemen sat on kit bags in the aisle. One man offered me a seat, because of my crutches, and Mam scowled at him and pushed past me to sit down. The man started to speak. "I'm fine standing," I said quickly. "With my crutches—"

I should have kept quiet. Mam's eyes narrowed. "I don't know who gave you the idea it was all right to go out where people could see you," she said, in a low, furious voice. "Flaunting your crippled self. You can use them things 'til we get home, and not a minute longer."

"But I can walk," I said.

"But I don't want you to. You hear me?"

I swallowed. It was worse than a nightmare.

"Ada caught a spy," Jamie whispered.

Mam snorted. "Pull the other one," she said.

"Tell her, Ada," Jamie said. "Tell her your hero story."

I kept my mouth shut and shook my head.

It was late at night before we got off the train, and went stumbling through the inky blacked-out streets of London. I tripped over rough curbstones. The shadows made noises I didn't remember, but the decaying smell rising from the damp streets was the same.

Butter, I thought. Think of riding Butter.

Mam had moved, she told us, to be closer to the factory where she now worked. "Plus it got me away from those titty-tatty neighbors with nothin' nice to say. I've got a decent job now, even if it is still nights. You'll like the new place. It won't be posh like that rich old bat's you were with, but it's pretty fine."

"Susan's not a rich old bat," Jamie said.

Oh, Jamie, I thought, shut up.

"Sure she is now. Bet she pockets what she gets

to take you in. Except, of course, for what she spent on those clothes. What's that you're wearing, anyhow, Ada? Pants?"

"Riding jodhpurs," I said, then immediately wished I hadn't.

"Oooh, fancy! What's that called, when it's at home?"

"They're just pants for riding," I said. "They're not posh. Posh ladies wear riding habits. And they didn't cost anything. Susan made them." She'd had to, when I'd worn out the pants Maggie gave me. And I should learn to shut up too, really I should.

"Ooh, posh ladies wear riding habits, do they? Surprised you ain't got one of those."

Susan had said she would make me one. She thought it would be fun.

"You won't be wearing pants in my house," Mam said. "Tomorrow I'll be taking those to the pawn shop and getting you something suitable. The cheek of her. Letting you out where people could see you."

"There's nothing much wrong with me," I said. "My foot's a long way from my brain."

Slap!

I fell backward, stumbling, scraping my elbow on something rough. For a moment I lost my crutches in the dark. Jamie helped me. Shut up, I thought. Shut up.

Mam led us up three flights of stairs. Bare dim

lightbulbs hung at each landing, throwing the stair-wells into shadow. I saw something scutter out of view. A rat, I thought. I'd forgotten rats. I'd forgotten how the hallways smelled from the common toilets on each floor.

Mam swung open a dirty wooden door. "Here we are," she said.

The flat was two small rooms. We walked into a room with a table, a sink, a gas ring, and some chairs. A thin rug on a linoleum floor.

No cabinet under the sink. No cabinet big enough to stuff me into. I looked first thing.

"Well?" Mam said.

I swallowed. "Very nice," I said.

"Posh brat," Mam said. "I can see I'm going to have to beat the toff outa you." She picked up one of the chairs near the table. "We'll put this right by the window," she said. "That way you'll be comfy, look-ing out."

What was I supposed to say? I no longer knew the right answers. "Thank you."

"I see we got Miss Manners living with us now. Thinks she's too good for the rest of us." Mam showed us the other room, containing our old wardrobe and a new bed. No sheets, just a rough blanket and a pillow and a mattress.

Until we'd gone to live with Susan, I was used to beds like this. I would have thought the flat was fine. Fancy, even, with more than one room.

"I had to take off work tonight to fetch you," Mam said. "I'm going down to the pub for a pint. You two better go to sleep. Ada, I'll find you a bucket."

It took me a moment to realize why she thought I needed a bucket. "I'd rather just use the toilet," I said. "I usually do now."

Mam said, each word heavy and solid, "You ain't going out of this room.

"Got that?" she continued. "'Cause I don't need the world shaming me for having a crippled girl. I don't care what you did somewhere else. You're with me again, you'll do as I say. You disobey me, I'll make you wish you hadn't. You're a cripple. That's all you are. A cripple, and nothing but a cripple. You've never been anything else. Got that?"

I said, "Susan wasn't ashamed of me."

"Well, bully for her. She should have been." Mam's eyes glittered. "Disobey me," she said, pointing at Jamie, "and I take it out on him. Got that?"

"Yes, ma'am," I said.

She went out. I looked at the door, and the bucket. I used the bucket.

Jamie and I lay on the mattress in the hot bedroom.

"I can't sleep," Jamie whimpered. "I need Bovril."

"Susan'll take good care of him," I whispered.

"I need him," Jamie said. "I can't sleep."

"I know," I said. "I know."

Jamie said, "What happened? Why's Mam so angry?"

"We look different," I said.

"So?"

I took a deep breath. Part of me felt like it was all my fault, for being too posh, for getting above myself, for not being the sort of daughter Mam could love.

For being a cripple.

And yet . . . Mam could have fixed my foot. She could have fixed it when I was a baby, and she could fix it now. She didn't want to.

She wanted me to be a cripple.

It didn't make sense.

The moon rose. I watched the patterns its light made on the ceiling. *A cripple, and nothing but a cripple.*

"Jamie," I said, poking him, "I caught a spy."

"I know," he said.

"And I learned to ride Butter, and we jumped the stone wall. Fred needs me."

"Mmmm," said Jamie, rolling over.

"And I can read and write, and knit, and sew. I

298

helped the soldiers during Dunkirk week. And Maggie and Daisy like me," I said.

"Susan loves you," Jamie said.

"She loves both of us," I said.

"I know," said Jamie. He sniffed. "I want Bovril."

I didn't reply. I drifted off to sleep, sometime before Mam came home, and as I did, I thought one word. *War.*

At last I understood what I was fighting, and why. And Mam had no idea how strong a fighter I'd become.

Chapter 43

In the morning Jamie had wet the bed. I'd half expected it, but Mam, sleeping on the other side of Jamie, was furious. She smacked his bottom hard and told him it'd better not happen again. "Else you'll sleep on the floor," she said.

Jamie sobbed. He wasn't used to being smacked anymore. "Quit crying," I whispered, my arms around him. "You've got to. Crying makes it worse." To Mam I said, "I'll wash the blanket." I reached to the floor for my crutches and my shoes.

They were gone.

Mam saw the look on my face. She laughed. "Missing your crutches, are you?"

"Why didn't you get me crutches when I was younger?" I asked.

Mam snorted. "I told you," she said. "I don't want you going anywhere. I don't want anyone to see you."

"But my foot could have been fixed. When I was a baby—"

"Oh, so now you believe all that too? That's what they said, those nurses, wanted me to spend money, wanted to take my baby and my money and put you in hospital for months, all my money, and nobody was going to tell me what to do with my money and my kid. Wouldn't have worked anyhow. When you was a baby your foot wasn't half as ugly as it is now."

I tried to absorb all this. But Jamie had thought of something else. "What about when the bombs come?" he asked. "Where'll we go then? At home we had a shelter—" He stopped, his eyes widening with fear. I understood. It was a mistake to call Susan's house *home*.

But Mam didn't notice. She just snorted. "Ain't no bombs in London," she said. "Haven't been, not once, and the war's been on a year."

It was a Saturday, but Mam said she'd be working that night. The factories ran around the clock. She dozed on the dry side of the bed while I toasted bread for breakfast and made tea. When she woke, she and Jamie went out to buy food. "Where're your ration cards?" Mam asked.

Susan had them. She would have given them to us,

if Mam hadn't been in such an all-fired hurry to leave.

I played dumb. "Dunno," I said. Jamie started to speak, but I glared at him and he closed his mouth on his words.

Mam swore. "That idiot woman," she said. "Probably trying to cheat me. Probably using all your coupons up right now, buying all the sugar and meat she can."

I said nothing. I went to the window, sat down on the chair, looked out. Nothing to see. No children playing in the streets. Sandbags up to the windows of the few shops. Women walking briskly, not sitting down on the stoops to gossip.

War.

Mam gave me a more congenial look. "You can't help it," she said, "but with a foot like that, there's nothing useful you can do. You'll be a cripple all your life."

When they left I became a spy. The flat was filthy, and I wanted to clean it, at the very least the sink and the floor, but I decided not to. Mam would notice and be angry. Better she thought I stayed in my chair.

There weren't many places to hide things. A few kitchen cupboards with the pots and plates Mam had had for years. Clothes in the wardrobe—new clothes, for Mam, and some older things too. A small table in the bedroom with a larger new mirror hung in front of it.

My hair looked a mess. I brushed it with Mam's hairbrush and plaited it neatly. My face was dirty, so I found a cloth and soap at the kitchen sink, and washed. I had to use the bucket again, but I moved it to the door and covered it with a plate to keep down the smell.

Back to the table with the mirror. It had a drawer. The front of the drawer was a mess of bobby pins, pencil stubs, and odd scraps of paper. I pulled it all the way out. At the very back I found a small pasteboard box. Inside, a stack of papers.

I unfolded the top one.

Certificate of Birth, it said. *Ada Maria Smith.*

I drew a deep breath. Scanned the paper quickly. Found what I was looking for. *May 13, 1929.*

We'd gotten my birthday wrong, of course, but we'd guessed right on the year. I really was eleven.

Jamie's birth certificate was beneath mine. Beneath that, my parents' marriage certificate.

I heard a loud noise on the stairs. Jamie singing at the top of his lungs. Beautiful, beautiful Jamie. By the time Mam swung the door open I had the papers back where they belonged and was sitting placidly in my chair.

For dinner Mam boiled potatoes and cabbage with a small piece of tough beef. She ate the beef herself, because, she said, until we had our ration books back we didn't have the right to eat meat. "I'll get that cat to send them," she said. "Get the law on her, if I have to."

Jamie looked miserable and didn't want to eat, but I piled his plate with vegetables. "They're good," I said encouragingly. "They tasted a little like the beef."

He eyed me. I winked. He stared at me for a while, then carefully ate everything on his plate.

When Mam got up to leave for work, I took a deep breath. It was time. *Now or never,* I thought. "You don't need us here," I said. "You're better off without having to take care of us, feed us and everything. You don't really want us. Not even Jamie."

Jamie started to say something, but I kicked him underneath the table, hard, and he shut his mouth.

Mam eyed me. "What's all this? Some kind of trick?"

"You never wanted us," I said. "Not really. That's why you didn't send for us, when all the other mothers did."

"Don't know what right you've got to complain about it," she said. "You had a pretty high time out there from all I can see. Fancy clothes, fancy ideas, prancing around the town—"

"It's nothing to you what happens to us," I said. "You only brought us back because you thought it would cost more to keep us away."

"And so it would have," Mam said. "You saw that letter. Why should I pay for you to live better than me? When you're nothing but a—"

"It doesn't matter," I said. I worked hard to keep my voice quiet and even. I was going to have the truth said plainly. I was done with lies.

"Nineteen shillings," Mam said. "Nineteen shillings a week! When they first let you go away for free. You never cost me no nineteen shillings a week. It's robbery, that's what it is."

"If you don't have to pay, you won't care if we leave," I said. "I can arrange that. We'll go away and you won't have to pay for anything."

Her eyes narrowed. "I don't know what you're up to, girl. I don't know where you got all these words. Talk, talk."

"I could get my foot fixed," I said. "Even now. I don't have to be a cripple. You don't have to be ashamed of me." A thought went through my head: *Susan isn't ashamed.*

Mam's face turned red. "I'm never paying to fix your foot."

"It would have been easy to fix, when I was a baby."

"Oh, that's lies! You can't believe what people say! Lies! I told your father—"

My father. I'd read about him in the newspaper

clipping in Mam's drawer. I said, slowly, "He would have fixed me." It was a guess.

"He wanted to," Mam said. "He was the one that wanted babies. It was him always rocking you, singing to you."

I felt tears dripping down my cheeks. I hadn't even realized I was crying. I said, "You never wanted us. You don't want us now."

Mam's eyes blazed. She said, "You're right, I don't."

"You never wanted us," I said.

"And why would I?" Mam said. "It was all him, calling me unnatural, wanting babies all the time. Then I got stuck with a cripple. And then a baby. And then no husband. *I never wanted either of you.*"

Jamie made a little noise. I knew he was crying but I couldn't look at him yet. I said, "So you don't need to keep us now. You won't have to pay. We'll be gone in the morning. We'll be gone for good."

Mam got up. She took her purse and hat. She turned back to look at me. "I can get rid of you without paying anything?"

I nodded.

She grinned. It was her stuffing-Ada-into-the-cabinet grin. "Is that a promise?" she said.

All of my life I would remember those words.

I said, "Yes."

Chapter 44

I held Jamie and we cried and cried. His tears wet the front of my shirt and my snot got into his hair. We cried like I'd never cried before.

It hurt so badly. The ache in my heart was worse than my foot had ever been.

When we stopped crying I held him in my arms and rocked him back and forth. At last he looked up at me, his lashes still fringed with tears. He said, "I want to go home."

"We are," I promised him. "As soon as the sun's up, we're going." I could read street signs now. I could find my way. I didn't have any money for a train fare, but I was willing to bet there would be a WVS post somewhere. The WVS women would help us out.

I got out the birth certificates and showed Jamie his. "You were born on November 29, 1933," I told him. "You are seven years old." I showed him the marriage certificate too. "Our father's name was James, just like yours."

And I took out the last piece of paper, a newspaper article. *Accident at Royal Albert Dock Kills Six.* "He died when you were a tiny baby. When I was just turned four."

I put the marriage certificate and the newspaper clipping back in the drawer, but stuffed the birth certificates into my jodhpur pocket, ready for the morning.

Whoop-WHOOP. Whoop-WHOOP. Whoop-WHOOP.

The sound came from the open window. Louder and louder.

An air raid.

I didn't know where the shelter was.

I didn't have crutches. I hadn't walked far on my bad foot for a long, long time.

Jamie grabbed my hand in panic. The siren's wail grew louder. "Come on!" I said.

"Where?"

I pretended I knew. "Down the stairs!" People were hurrying out of the flats, rushing down with bedding in their arms. I couldn't slide down the stairs, not in the crowd, so I clutched the rail with both hands and went as fast as I could while people pushed past me. Jamie held on to my shirt, trembling. The siren began to wind down, its noise replaced by far-off blasts.

Bombs.

Out in the dark street, I couldn't see where to go.

I could hear people, but they seemed to be moving in all directions. Shouts echoed between the buildings. I grabbed Jamie's hand and turned at random, moving as fast as I could. An open doorway, a stair going down—anything—

A bomb exploded overhead. The streets rang with the sound of shattering glass. Far in front of us, toward the docks, the sky began to glow red. Fire. The docks were on fire.

A building behind us exploded. The shock wave threw us into the street. My ears felt like they'd exploded too. Bricks rained down, and pieces of glass and rubble. I put my arms over Jamie's head. He looked like he was screaming, but I couldn't hear him. I couldn't hear anything.

I scrambled to my feet, pulling him with me. There in front of us was an open door. Steps leading down. A shelter. Thank God.

Strangers hauled us inside. Down the stairs to a basement room full of people, hot and damp. Concerned faces, lips moving, saying things I couldn't hear. Hands holding us up, cradling us, offering us tea. Wiping blood from Jamie's face. Wiping my face as well.

People made room for us on the concrete floor. Someone wrapped a blanket around us. I hung on to Jamie. I would never let go of him, I thought. Never.

Chapter 45

Eventually we slept. In the morning an air raid warden roused us all. "The fires are getting closer," he said. "We've got to clear everyone out."

I sat up. The docks had been on fire. But they were a long way off. Weren't they?

It wasn't until the man answered me, saying, "All sorts of stuff is on fire, miss. The water mains are broken and they're having a time getting the blazes out," that I realized I had spoken. Then I realized I could hear. My ears still rang, but they were working again.

I shook Jamie. He emerged from sleep like a rabbit from a burrow, a tiny bit at a time. "I want to go home," he said.

I nodded. "Yes."

He was gray with dust from head to toe. Smears of red from his bloody nose still ran across his neck. His shirt was torn and he was missing a shoe. I supposed I looked as bad, or worse. "Come on," I said.

We emerged onto the ruined street, where gaps showed in the rows of buildings like missing teeth. A pall of dust and smoke choked the sunlight, but the street sparkled as though covered with stars. Glass. All the shattered glass.

And coming toward us, picking her way through the rubble and debris, a small figure with frizzy blond hair poking out the sides of her hat. She looked like a thin, very determined witch. I stared, disbelieving. My voice dried up in my mouth.

Not Jamie. "Susan!" he screamed.

Her head snapped up as if yanked by a string. Her mouth flew open, and then she was running toward us, and Jamie was running, knocking into her, burying his filthy face in her skirt, and then I caught up, and before I knew it her arms were around me too. Her wool cardigan felt scratchy against my face. I put my arms around her, over the top of Jamie's head. I held on tight.

"Oh, my dears," she said. "What a disaster. What a miracle. You're all right. You're both all right."

Chapter 46

A restaurant near the train station was open despite having had its windows blown out. Susan ordered tea, then took us to the loo and tried to clean us up. "Where are your crutches?" she asked me. "Oh, Ada, your poor feet." Despite my stockings, my feet were covered with cuts. "What happened to your shoes?"

"Mam took them," I said. "And then I couldn't get to the shelter fast enough. Not before the first bombs fell."

She pressed her lips together, but didn't speak. Back in our seats she continued to sit silently. A waitress brought us sandwiches and we began to eat.

"How did you find us?" Jamie asked.

"Your mother left her letters behind. One of them had her address on it. But that building—" She paused. "Well, it took a hit, I'm afraid. But some of the people who lived there had come back, were standing by the rubble this morning, and one woman thought she remembered seeing you going down the stairs."

Susan made a face. "She remembered passing you, because you were moving so slowly. So I hoped you'd made it to a shelter. I've been searching the shelters. I never realized there'd be so many."

I had a more important question. "Why? Why did you come for us, after you let us go?"

Susan stirred her tea with a spoon, round and round, looking thoughtful. The restaurant had sugar on the table, but it was bad manners to take more than a bit. "You'll find out," she said at last, "that there are different kinds of truth. It's true your mother has a right to you. I was thinking of that when I let you go.

"But then I couldn't sleep. I sat in the shelter with the wretched cat and I realized that no matter what the rules were, I should have kept you. Because it was also true that you belonged to me. Do you understand that? Can you?"

I said, "We were coming back to you this morning."

She nodded. "Good."

A few minutes later she added, "I took the first train I could, yesterday. But it was so slow, and it stopped so many times, and then when the bombing started they wouldn't keep going into London. We spent most of the night on a siding, and only pulled into the station at dawn."

She stopped talking. Jamie had slumped against the table. He was sound asleep.

Susan held my arm as I limped to the station. She said, "You needed new crutches anyhow. You were getting too tall for your old ones."

I nodded, grateful I didn't have to explain. Someday I'd tell her the whole story, what I'd said to Mam and what she'd said to me, but not now. Maybe not for a long time. It tore a hole through my heart just to think about it.

The train to Kent was packed. Susan found a seat for me, but Jamie ended up lying down beneath the benches and Susan sat on a soldier's bag in the aisle. The train moved in fits and starts; I dozed with my head against the wall. When Jamie had to use the toilet, soldiers passed him over their heads to the one at the end of the car, and back again when he was done.

When we stumbled out of the station at our village, Susan waved toward the taxi parked by the curb. "Get in," she said to me. "I'm not making you walk another step."

We drove through the quiet Sunday morning village and down Susan's tree-lined drive. Suddenly, she gasped.

I got out of the taxi, and saw what she saw.

The house was gone.

A direct hit from a German bomb.

What seemed like half the village stood among the rubble, carefully lifting away bricks and stones. They looked up at the taxi.

They saw us, and it was like when we saw Susan in London all over again, the astonishment on their faces. The fear turning to happiness, to laughter and smiles.

Susan stood frozen, her hand covering her mouth.

They rushed toward us—Fred, the vicar, Stephen White. The publican and his wife. The policemen. Pilots. Lady Thorton threw her arms around Susan and burst into tears.

"Why didn't you tell me you were leaving?" she sobbed. "You never go anywhere—why didn't you let anyone know?"

A blur of gray fur streaked out of the rubble straight toward Jamie. "Bovril!" he shrieked.

The pasture lay beyond the rubble. I tried to run, but after three steps Fred caught me. "He's fine," he said. "Your pony's fine. He must have been on the other side of the field when the bomb hit." Tears were coursing down Fred's cheeks. "It's you we were missing," he gasped. "You we were digging for. The sirens never went off last night. We thought we'd lost all three of you."

Jamie bounced over to Susan, grinning. "We've been shipwrecked," he said.

Susan still looked stunned, but at Jamie's insistence she stroked Bovril's head. Then she put her arms around Jamie and looked directly at me. "It's lucky I went after you," she said. "The two of you saved my life, you did."

I slipped my hand into hers. A strange and unfamiliar feeling ran through me. It felt like the ocean, like sunlight, like horses. Like love. I searched my mind and found the name for it. *Joy.* "So now we're even," I said.